17.95

D0344333

OFFICIALLY
WITHDRAWN

THE
SECOND WAR

THE
SECOND WAR

G. C. HENDRICKS

VIKING

VIKING
Published by the Penguin Group
Viking Penguin, a division of Penguin Books USA Inc.,
40 West 23rd Street, New York, New York 10010, U.S.A.
Penguin Books Ltd, 27 Wrights Lane,
London W8 5TZ, England
Penguin Books Australia Ltd, Ringwood,
Victoria, Australia
Penguin Books Canada Ltd, 2801 John Street,
Markham, Ontario, Canada L3R 1B4
Penguin Books (N.Z.) Ltd, 182–190 Wairau Road
Auckland 10, New Zealand

Penguin Books Ltd, Registered Offices:
Harmondsworth, Middlesex, England

First published in 1990 by Viking Penguin,
a division of Penguin Books USA Inc.

1   3   5   7   9   10   8   6   4   2

Copyright © G. C. Hendricks, 1990
All rights reserved

LIBRARY OF CONGRESS CATALOGING IN PUBLICATION DATA
Hendricks, G. C.
The second war / G. C. Hendricks.
p.   cm.
ISBN 0-670-83018-6
I. Title.
PS3558.E49517S44   1990
813′ .54—dc20   89-40315

Printed in the United States of America
Set in Primer
Designed by Ellen Levine

For Laurel Goldman and
Robin Cartwright Hendricks

The author gratefully acknowledges the advice and assistance of Peggy Payne, Linda Orr, Angela Davis-Gardner, Peter Filene, Georgeann Eubanks, Carrie Knowles, Jack Raper, Dick Elam, Marilyn Dunigan, William Price Fox, Betty Adcock, Peggy Hoffman, Miriam Sauls, Linda Gupton, Ed Osborne, Pam Fitts, Donia Steele, Joan Agnor, Rhoda Weyr, Susan Moldow, and those responsible for the Short Course Program at Duke University Continuing Education.

BOOK ONE

THE PREPARATION

HEPZEBIAH
OCTOBER 1960

The junior varsity football team at Piedmont School was awful. Only seventeen boys dressed out for practice, and on Thursday nights a few of them had to work, helping with tobacco and harvesting corn in the fall and beans in the early winter. The team lost football games for six years, but we youngsters joined the band so we could go to the games and see our friends somewhere besides at school, and we had our heroes, the ones we wanted to be like when it came our time to play.

We were all poor but did not know it because we ate good food and we had the church. There was a girl who lived in Hepzebiah Community, down the dirt road, past the creek. I was in the seventh grade when I noticed her. I spent all my free time thinking about Judy, waiting sometimes for hours so I could see her, knowing she liked to walk in the evenings on the dirt road with her daddy; and I hung out at school in places I knew I would see her. Her eyes were drawn at the corners, like an Asian cat's, and her hair was long and black and straight. She had a dimple on each cheek. I played clarinet in junior band and Judy was a flag bearer. When there was a junior varsity away game we put on our band uniforms and rode the bus with the junior varsity football players.

3

Judy wore a short, pleated skirt, with her knees showing beneath, and a heavy sweater with a "P" on the front, and thick white socks rolled down. Everybody talked on the bus except the driver. I tried to talk to Judy, but we couldn't sit together because of the rules: no shouting, no chewing gum, no talking to the driver, no switching seats, and no boys and girls sitting together.

One school we played against was in the country. The field where the game was played had been pasture. It was rough and was not level, but they had a new lighting system they dedicated that night to a teacher who had died. There was a set of grey bleachers, metal frames and wooden seats, where fans and the bands from both schools sat, and people were standing all around the field at the edge. The band had special seats in the bleachers. I managed to sit with Judy since there were no rules in the bleachers. Before the game started an announcer spoke over a sound system that made his voice ring. The chill of fall held mist in the air. A lot of people were smoking, and smoke hung in the mist. The announcer told us that the teacher who had died taught two generations of people from their community and that there were very few people around who had not felt this man's influence. He asked us to have a moment of silence for the man who had died, and all of us in the bleachers and all the people around the edge of the field stood still in the new light and bowed our heads while everybody was silent. Then the announcer said "Amen" and a referee blew his whistle. Our director lifted his baton, and the junior band played a march, sitting in the bleachers, while Judy and the other flag bearers ran onto the field and twirled their flags. When we finished playing the march some of the people in the bleachers sat down. Other people kept standing and shouted at their children or friends on the field. Judy put her flag down and came and sat with me. She was excited; her lower jaw shivered from the chilly air, but her eyes were on the field. The players were huddled and praying, getting ready.

The first half was a series of three downs and a punt. The band performed at halftime and played a weak song with Judy and the other flag bearers out front. Not long into the second half a boy who was my hero, an eighth grader named Lewis, scored a touchdown. He was tall and thin with a crew cut and he always hustled. He put his head down and ran straight ahead. Judy and I bought drinks at halftime, and we spilled them when Lewis scored the touchdown. Judy hugged me, jumping up and down. We screamed for a while after each play. After a while we did not scream so much but stayed standing for the rest of the game. When we clapped, our arms rubbed against each other. I felt her body, inside the sweater, when she rubbed against my arm. Lewis's score was the only one. By the time the referees blew the game over, everybody from Piedmont was shouting and talking about it being the first time in over six years our boys had won a game.

Because Piedmont won, they changed the rules and allowed shouting on the bus on the way home, but I couldn't sit with Judy because of the other rules. The bus got quiet during the long drive home. It was after eleven when we got back to our part of the county. The coach was driving. He was supposed to take everybody as close to their homes as he could get, but he changed the rules and dropped us off at the end of our dirt road, where it runs into Snakey Road, in Hepzebiah Community. He told us we would have to walk down the dirt road because he had to have everybody else home by midnight.

The bus pulled away and left us in its fumes. We looked at each other and smiled. I told Judy I would walk her home. The moon was out and some low clouds were blowing by fast. We had a mile to walk to Judy's house, past Uncle Goody's cabin, where the sexton always lived, with the hog pen and smokehouse out back, and past the church and the parsonage, then across the creek.

When we started walking Judy said she was cold. I hugged her. She twisted away from me and squealed, "We won!" Her face was flushed, and her white wool uniform was bright in the light from the moon. We walked side by side.

I said, "I knew when Lewis got away from that last tackler he was gone. Did you see that last tackler?"

"I saw him running down the field. I'll never forget him running down that field."

In the fields on both sides of the road, rows of soybean plants with their leaves and pods dried close to the stalks were rustling in the light breeze. The road ditches and ditch bank were covered by dried weeds and dried wildflowers.

"You're different," I said.

"Different from what?"

"The other girls are always saying I'm the preacher's boy."

"They're just joshing, Horace."

"We stole a car."

Judy stopped, and I stopped beside her.

"Mister Alcie Pace's Studebaker," I said. "Me and Charlie. Mister Alcie was gone to the beach fishing. We took the Studebaker out and ran Snakey Road."

Judy turned toward the creek and started walking fast.

I followed her. "We went to his house and Charlie straightwired the Studebaker. He drove it as fast as he could on Snakey Road." I was walking beside Judy explaining.

"My daddy used to run Snakey Road, but it was dirt then and the cars didn't have big engines."

"Charlie drove crazy. We skidded around those curves before you get to the bottom. All I could think about was we had stole that car."

"How'd you get out of the parsonage without your momma finding out?"

"I snuck out and met Charlie. We'd talked about it at school. Tried to get Earl to go with us, but he wouldn't do it."

Judy was walking down the dirt road toward the creek, listening to me.

"Let's do something," I said.

She socked me on the arm and started running toward the creek. The light wind was mild. I started running too. The road was smooth in spite of lumps of gravel left by the man from the state with his diesel scraper, and it was dry and it was hard to get traction on the loose gravel. I slid a few times on the gravel, then ran and caught up with Judy, and then passed her on a run. Her hair was flowing behind her like a mule's tail. We passed Uncle Goody's place in a dead run. Then the church was on the right, bold in the blue-white light that angled off the clapboards, light from the moon against the black piney woods. I passed the church driveway, running in front of Judy, and pointed toward the church. I stopped. I stopped Judy when she caught up with me.

"Let's ring the bell," I said.

I was holding her shoulders, looking at her. She was breathing hard.

"We can't ring the bell." She stood still and let me hold her shoulders.

"Uncle Goody told me every time Piedmont won a game, back after the war, whoever went from Hepzebiah would come and ring the bell, then they'd go outside and do some cheers, then they'd all go to somebody's house and get something to eat."

"You're not supposed to ring the bell unless there's church."

I left her standing and ran toward the church; then I heard her behind me and turned to see. She was right behind me and she was racing. She whispered loud running past me, grunting with each step, "We'll wake everybody up!"

We ran onto the grass in front of the black-and-white hand-painted sign that read HEPZEBIAH BAPTIST CHURCH. FOUNDED 1860. REVEREND HORACE A. HARDY, SENIOR, PASTOR. We stopped running. The church clapboards were white with black shadow streaks, and the oaks in the churchyard and the windows of the church were dark. At the base of the white steeple, before it started narrowing, was a dark open space where you could see the black iron wheels that rolled the bell. The steeple threw a black shadow across the brick walk. We were both out of breath.

"We won!" I said.

"Is it locked?"

"Uncle Goody doesn't lock it until right before he goes to bed."

"They'll come and get us," Judy said, and she looked at me, then she looked at the church, then down the dirt road toward her house and the creek. She was breathing hard. "Okay, Horace. But we'd better not get in trouble."

We looked around to see if anybody was watching and tiptoed quietly up the brick steps. The large, plain door was unlocked and did not squeak. It was dark in the vestibule, and I switched on the light and squinted. A streak was lit into the little room off the vestibule, and a rope hung from the bell in the steeple through a small, vertical tunnel into the unpainted, wood-walled room; the knot at the end of the rope hung still.

"You want to go first?" I whispered.

Judy had her hands on her hips. "Sure." She marched into the wood-walled room and pulled lightly on the rope, looking up the tunnel at the darkness. Then she came back toward me and licked the fingers on her right hand and stuck her hand out toward me, palm up. I licked my fingers and we stared into each other's eyes, and we touched hands.

Then she turned and she grabbed the rope with both hands and said, "I always wanted to ring this thing."

I had rung the bell a few times on Sunday mornings when Uncle Goody was ringing it. He would tell me I had to get the rhythm so it wouldn't work me, so I could let it do the work. I did not want to teach Judy how to ring the bell. I wanted to ring it. Judy jerked up some the first few times the rope rose. Then she figured out how to do it, and I wanted us both to ring it. The first clap was a soft, dull thud. When Judy picked up the rhythm and the clapper swung back, the bell sang a full tone. I watched her from the doorway. I had my arms folded and was leaning against the jamb. She moved with the rope, pulling, rising, steadier as she went, landing in the streak of light in position to pull. When she landed with her arms up her sweater pulled tight against her breasts. She rang for a while, biting her lower lip, pulling and grunting, with me watching. The sound of the ring was muffled through the little tunnel where the rope hung, not like the pure echoes of our voices from the sanctuary or the clear tolling from outside. We heard the sound from all around every time she landed hard with her legs wrapped around the rope.

"Somebody ought to be here by now," she said.

As I watched her my heart beat hard. I was afraid she would hear it. "I'll ring," I said. "I never rung at night. In the daytime you can see sunlight coming down through that little tunnel where the rope goes up."

"How long will it take them to come?"

I stretched my arms over my head and loosened my shoulders. "I'll ring." I walked into the streak of light where she stood.

Judy went down hard with the rope, pulling straight down. I put my hands on the rope above hers and we went up with the rope into the darkness at the top of the room. Her heavy sweater smelled musty from sweat and her neck smelled sweet like flowers. Our bodies were together, both arms, both legs, and our faces were on opposite sides of the rope, inches apart. I felt her breath. She stuck out her tongue. As the rope came down I landed in position to pull and she landed stiff-kneed. She rushed aside and sat in a straight, wooden chair and looked at her hands.

"Mister Alcie Pace told me they just use those chairs at homecoming and funerals. He gave them to the church," I said. The rope moved into the dark tunnel as I rose. The room smelled like pine pitch and varnish.

"I know that." Judy looked at her hands. "I got blisters."

"From just that?"

"I rang it a long time."

"Thought you worked in tobacco."

"I did."

"Why ain't your hands tough?"

"I'm a girl."

We listened to the tolling while I rang. I breathed in rhythm to the ringing.

"Uncle Goody told me when Piedmont won a game and rang the bell some of the ladies would come to the church, like Miss Nellie or Miss Grace when they were younger, and one of them would always ask everybody over to their house. Uncle Goody said they would let him come."

"He's been in our house." She was still looking at her hands.

"Momma always feeds him on Saturdays because he's doing the yard. She feeds him on the porch, but I've seen him in the parsonage when he fixed our stove."

"My daddy lets him eat at the table."

"Momma lets his younguns eat at the table in the kitchen," I said. "Mister Alcie Pace lets him eat at his grill."

The rope was hemp, smooth and oily where I held it, rough and stringy up higher. Judy wiggled in the chair, moving around, changing the way she sat. Her hands stayed busy with her hair. I saw this from my crouch-and-pull on the floor, in the streak of light, and from my stretch-and-rise-with-the-rope in the darkness of the high part of the room, and from all the space in between. She would glance up when I went up, then look at her hands when I went down.

We heard clicking and a slow shuffle on the brick steps, and the latch on the inside of the big door in the vestibule flipped.

"Shit!" I said.

Judy looked at me. "Who is it?"

"I don't know."

"What will they do?"

I kept ringing and whispered, "We won."

Uncle Goody came through the big door. "Whut th' Sam Hill you younguns doing?"

"We won the ball game," I said.

The bare bulb hanging from the high ceiling in the vestibule reflected off the oily black skin of his bald head, and the light cast a shadow over the grey beard on his chin and the bottom parts of his cheeks. He closed the door behind him and walked toward us. His shirt was pale blue with dark pinstripes, open at the collar. The overalls were worn, patched and clean. He was bent and leaning as he walked.

Judy sat up straight in her chair, watching him come.

"Rings true, don't she?" He smiled and looked up the tunnel toward the bell that was now still but still humming. Then he told us my daddy had to go out because there had been a shooting, and Momma and Beth were at the parsonage scared and wondering where I was, and Judy's daddy had come looking for her earlier.

I had stopped ringing. "Who's shooting?"

"Don' know. Yo' daddy went."

Judy stood and walked past Uncle Goody, out of the wood-walled room and into the vestibule, into the light, toward the door. "I thought people were supposed to come."

"Wuz a time when they did," Uncle Goody said. "They all busy now. 'Sides, you-uns is junior vars'ty."

We left the church with Uncle Goody, cutting out the light, and he locked the door. We walked all the way to Judy's house, a half-mile across the creek, and nobody talked. On the way back the last of the lightning bugs at the creek were glimmering on the ground, not able to fly. Uncle Goody went to his place behind the church where the sexton always stays and made sure Son had not rolled off the porch, and I went home to the parsonage. Momma and Beth were scared. They didn't know why the bell had been ringing. They hugged me when I came in and Momma bolted the doors. A black man and a white man had shot each other and both of them died, and Daddy stayed out all night with the families.

PARRIS ISLAND
OCTOBER 1966

When we were in boot camp we all wanted to be fighting marines like the drill instructors and other men we saw around the base who had been to Vietnam, and we wanted to get that way fast. When my platoon got assigned to a week's mess duty, we complained to each other when nobody was looking because if the drill instructors saw us talking they would hit us in the stomachs, even if we were talking about wanting to be fighting marines.

We marched from the barracks to the chow hall every morning at three. I was the guide, the fellow who carries the flag in front of the formation, and when we were marching to the chow hall in the dark the drill instructor would sometimes let me call the cadence.

"Howcum you get to call the cadence? Don' nobody else get to call the cadence."

Ely was from Louisiana. Ely was a squad leader and I was the guide. He was black, what everybody around home used to call a "blue gum," and his front teeth were gold. His wide forehead and nose and lips were accentuated by the shaven head. His eyes showed a natural brightness, all that was left of a smile he couldn't show at boot camp. His muscular arms and chest bulged under his utility shirt.

They told me and Ely to peel potatoes. Sometimes the drill instructors needed us to run errands. We could stop peeling and run the errands and come back and start peeling again easier than we could pull off any other job at the chow hall. It was a job that never ended.

The spud locker was a raised-concrete abutment at the back of the building, a part of the back dock, between the raw-garbage bins and the walk-in freezer. It was enclosed by chicken wire and screen stretched on two-by-four studs. We had two old metal folding chairs that were stamped "Special Services" but had been discarded. We had on white utilities with short sleeves and little white hats and combat boots.

I had learned the way to peel a potato and finish with the peel in one piece: you make a streak over the area with the most eyes and follow the pattern of the streak. I had finished three peels in a row using the streak method when Ely asked me why I got to call cadence, and since it was the first thing he had ever said to me in a normal voice, without whispering, I took a chance and spoke.

"Sergeant Servantes called me into his office one day and told me I sure do march pretty, and asked me if I could carry a flag without dropping it. I told him yeah—I mean, I told him 'Yes, sir'—about five times."

Ely grinned. "Where'dya learn to march so pretty?" He was slicing slabs off the sides of the spuds and putting the peels in a pot.

"I just feel the cadence."

Ely sliced for a few minutes then started whistling some low jazz. He was jamming, making up the stuff as he went along. Then he switched to birdcalls and he sounded like real birds. The faint echo of the whistling rose over the knocking noise of the refrigeration compressors and the humming of the cooling fans. The echo bounced off a row of dumpsters beyond a gravel parking lot behind the dock.

The drill instructor slipped into view a few feet outside the screen. His campaign hat was low over his eyes. His uniform was immaculate. His hands were clasped behind his back. I jumped up at attention, with a potato in one hand and a knife in the other. Ely turned and saw the drill instructor and jumped up at attention.

Sergeant Servantes spoke quietly. "The only two things in the world that whistle are boatswain's mates and cocksuckers, and I haven't seen any boatswain's mates around here." He looked at the sacks of potatoes and the pots. "Hardy!"

"Sir!" I was frozen in place.

"That you whistlin'?"

"No, sir!"

"Think you can get this cocksuckin' nigger to stop whistlin'?"

"Yes, sir!"

Sergeant Servantes stood outside the screen, watching.

I looked into Ely's bright eyes. Ely was watching me too.

"Take that cover off and get down!" I spoke in my new military voice.

He dropped the potato he was holding into the sack in front of him and removed his white hat and dropped it beside his chair, then walked two steps to an open part of the concrete floor. He went down into the push-up position with his face staring directly into a shined brass drain.

I looked at Sergeant Servantes. He was standing at parade rest, and he was smiling.

"How many can you do, Ely?" I asked.

"Don' know, Guide."

"Let's find out."

He bent his arms and lowered his body until his nose touched the drain; then he stiffened his arms and pushed his body up. The toes of his boots held his feet vertical, and his back was straight. He went down again. Sergeant Servantes held his place. I sat in the folding chair and started peeling a potato. "You counting?" I asked.

Ely pushed away from the drain and looked toward me. "Nineteen." Then he went down.

I cut a streak of peel around a bunch of eyes that were close together but the peel broke off, so I started slicing just to get rid of the potato.

The drill instructor spoke from outside the screen. "Guide!"

I jumped to attention and shouted, "Yes, sir!"

"He's not learning anything except how to do push-ups."

"Sir! The private requests—"

"Do it, Guide!"

"Sir!"

"Fucking *do* it!"

I went to Ely and stood over him with one boot at each of his shoulders.

"How many, Ely?"

He was sweating and his voice was strained. "Sixty-four!"

I put my right boot on his back, just behind his head, and pressed down. Ely hesitated; then he overcame the pressure and pushed himself up until his arms were straight, his muscles bulging.

"Sixty-five!"

He made it to seventy. I looked through the screen. Sergeant Servantes nodded, encouraging. I put most of my weight on Ely when he went down, and he couldn't lift his face away from the drain.

"You gonna whistle anymore, Ely?"

"No, Guide!" He was straining to push up.

I brought my left boot over so I was standing on his back, on the broad part of his shoulders.

"You gonna whistle anymore, Ely?" I balanced myself on his back.

"No, Guide."

He stopped trying to push up and held just enough pressure to keep my weight from crushing him into the concrete. I stomped him with my left boot, like marking time or stomping a butt, then walked back to my chair and started peeling.

"You make sure he doesn't whistle anymore, Guide," Sergeant

Servantes said. We heard his crisp, regular footsteps as he walked away, around the corner of the building, out of view of the back dock.

Ely pushed himself away from the floor and came to his feet and brushed himself off. He looked at me he and stretched his arms out to his sides, loosening his muscles. He went to his seat and sat on the front edge of his chair, limp, leaning forward, breathing hard, with his hands dangling. He picked up his knife. He tossed the knife straight up. It twisted and flopped end over end in the air. He caught the knife by the handle with the blade pointed out. He started peeling. After some time Ely raised the hand with the knife in it and rubbed the back of his wrist and forearm across his brow and down his chin, wiping sweat; then he went back to work.

The compressors on the back dock were pumping away with knocks at different speeds, and there was the constant background hissing and the humming of the fans. Some of the belts on the fans squeaked because the pulleys were out of round and the belts were not able to run true.

"Heard from home?" I whispered.

He didn't look up.

I tried again. "How's your folks?"

Ely kept peeling and looked at me.

"Ain't got no folks."

Ely got the last potato out of the sack, and I threw that sack into a hamper, got a full sack off a pallet next to the wall, put the full sack between our seats, and opened it and sat.

"You play ball?"

Ely leaned back and stretched his neck, looking in both directions through the screen, then he spoke: "Guard an' linebacka."

"Y'all any good?"

Ely looked out the screen in both directions again. "We wuz the smallest grade-B team in the state, an' we won the title two years runnin'."

"Play basketball?"

"Had to work in the dead o'winter. Had to hep my granddaddy on the bayous."

"Doing what?"

"Catchin' alligators t'sell, an' fish, an' anythin' else we come up on. Weren't no time to go to school in the dead o'winter."

"They let you play ball?"

"I could whip your white little ass." He picked up another potato.

"You ain't gonna whistle anymore, are you, Ely?"

"An' I could kill that bastard out there." When he smiled, his gold teeth shined.

"But you ain't gonna whistle anymore, are you?"

"Naw, Guide. I ain't gonna whistle no mo'."

TEXAS
APRIL 1969

I met Pete at flight school. He was from the Naval Academy. He was stocky, athletic. He had played some football, and he always stood and walked erect. I never saw him lean on anything when he was standing; he always kept his own space and carried his own weight. His head was shaved every day, just like mine, but I had come through the ranks. We were both in advanced jets. We were at the officers' club bar drinking Jack Daniel's when we met, and we talked about camping. We decided to go camping the next weekend.

On Saturday night we drove his Corvette to a grove of isolated cottonwoods on a small, fast-moving creek in the Texas hills. It was still cold at night. The night came early. We had the place to ourselves. About dusk, while we sipped beers in the quiet after cooking fish over the fire, a breeze came from the southwest. Pete had done most of the cooking. He had used two iron skillets. It was a dry wind that made the cottonwoods twist and bend. The trees shuddered as each wind came through in waves. When the wind got strongest, we moved below the edge of the creek bank, down to the water, to get out of the wind. The trees were swaying in the wind gusts, rotating their limbs like they were doing

warm-ups before a game. Pete knelt in the edge of the creek with
the skillets and washed them with sand. He used a clump of moss
from the creek to scrub the sand in the skillets until no grease
showed in the water. I watched from out of the wind. When he
finished washing the skillets we stayed in the creek bed out of the
wind. Low cirrostratus clouds were coming out of the southwest,
moving with the wind. As the intensity of the wind increased, the
dead limbs from the winter fell from the trees. The new leaves
brushed together to make a sound like an engine, a deep, throaty
roar in the background like a jet engine that came and went as
the wind gusted. The moon was big and orange to the east. It
came with the dark and threw crisp shadows through the gaps in
the moving clouds, so moonlight streaks crept on the ground
from the southwest. The streaks were filtered more by the trees.
The moonlight was broken into little pieces before it got to us in
the creek bed.

When we were on the flight schedule we had to get up at
four-thirty to be at the flight line by six. On the way to the flight
line we stopped at the officers' club, at the back entrance to the grill
where the chow line formed, cafeteria style. It was where
everybody in their flight suits with patches on their sleeves waited
for their morning visit with Maria. The rest of the officers' club was
empty, closed in the mornings.

"Know what you want? You awake?" Maria would ask in her
thick Mexican accent. We moved through the line as Maria filled
each order. "You can't fly those jets without guts," she would say,
"and you ain't got no guts unless you eat one of Maria's famous
western omelets." The heat lamps and lights and gas-fired grill
made the place bright and warm. Maria always said something
different to each of us. She never remembered what to call us,
though our names were stenciled on tape over our hearts. "You
can't drink beer until late at night, and eat my food, and fly jets,
flyboy. You've got to give up one of them." When she said that, we

all shouted, "Guess what we're gonna give up, Maria?" and she would throw back her fat head and laugh. She would ask about our women. "You're going to forget how to do with women," she would say. "You spend all your time with them airplanes. I got this pretty niece, but I tell her to stay away from the flyboys."

Pete's favorite thing was to slip through the line and go behind the counter and flip on the radio that played Mexican music. Maria would slap at Pete with her spatula and put her hand on her big hip and glare at him. She had hairnets of all colors and seemed to have some pattern in the order she chose to wear them—white, grey, red, green, then white again, then some random grouping for about a week, then back to the white, grey, red, and green—and all the hairnets mashed her greasy black hair against her fat head. She wore an apron that made her look fatter. Her skin was like chocolate, so she couldn't blush. She never stopped smiling. The only thing she would let anybody get by with behind her counter was when Pete slipped back there and flipped on the radio.

The radio news at five-thirty was brought to us by the Gomez Funeral Parlor. During the first commercial break, at five-thirty-five, a man with a Mexican accent and a soft voice would say, "Welcome to the Obituary of the Air," and a tinny electric organ would start playing a favorite hymn, a song everybody knew. Then the man would read the names and the vital information about the people the Gomez Funeral Parlor was handling. "Raul Raimarez, sixty-four, of two-thirteen Rio Verde Avenue, died Tuesday. He is survived by his wife, Sonora, and their children: Raul, nineteen; Jesus, seventeen; Maria, fifteen; Carlota, thirteen; Amelia, eleven; Jose, nine; Juan, seven; Sagarita, five; and Margarita, three." The man would say when the service would be. If more than one person had died, the Gomez Funeral Parlor commercial lasted longer than the news. Maria was always quiet during the commercial, though she kept cooking the omelets and orders of eggs and hash browns and occasionally some grits.

Sometimes the man in the commercial would say, "Welcome to

the Obituary of the Air," and the organ would play the hymn and he would say, "No deaths today." When that happened we'd all jump up in the middle of eating, and rush out, grabbing our flight bags on the way, gobbling the last of our eggs and hash browns and shouting, "No deaths today! No deaths today!"

The officers' club was by the bay, not far from the water. It was old and brick and elegant, worn by years of naval aviators. In the front of the club, near the main entrance, was the bar. The bar was all wood and leather. The walls of the bar were lined with squadron emblems. Among the emblems were pictures of ships and the men who worked on them and pictures of airplanes and groups of sailors and pilots formally posed in uniforms.

Pete and I went to the bar every night; we always wore our cowboy shirts and jeans. Girls from all the towns near the base came to the bar to get picked up, but the girls who worked at the bar were the hardest to get. When a new girl worked the bar, the first one to see her would call tallyho. I would say, "Tallyho on the long brown hair at nine o'clock," and Pete would order the drinks, and the girl would bring them and Pete would pay for the drinks, and I owned the first line because I had seen her first and called tallyho.

One night when Pete and I went to the bar there was a new girl. She was wearing a high-necked blouse, button-up, with three-quarter sleeves, and a full skirt and sneakers. Her skin and face were clean, fresh.

I called tallyho and asked her, "You ever been to Chicago?"

She smiled and picked up some empty beer glasses. "No." She spoke pure Southern. She walked toward the other end of the bar, where flight students and naval aviators were drinking beer and whiskey and playing dice games and moving their hands through the air, telling stories about flying airplanes.

"That's a shitty line," Pete said.

"Figured nobody had ever asked her that before."

He said, "She's tough."

"I like her."

"You don't deserve anything nice as she is."

"I bet she is nice."

"Bet you fuck her," he said.

"Uncle Goody used to tell me men was animals."

"And?"

"Don't want any tonight."

"Bet she could get you interested."

"I think she's nice."

"Probably fuck your eyes out. Every airplane driver in the free world's tried her."

"She's new here," I said.

We sipped our beers, occasionally glancing at the girl waiting on other fliers at the bar.

I asked Pete, "You ever been to Chicago?"

"Been to Paris. Went there when I was a second classman." Pete took his last sip of beer and held the heavy glass up to his left eye and squinted the uncovered eye, looking at the bar through the bottom of the glass. "Distorted colors, indistinguishable shapes that move." He smiled. "Just like Singapore. Went there when I was a first classman. Paris looked the same as Singapore and this place here." He set the glass on the bar and caught the girl's attention and held up two fingers. "Every bar in every town at every port in the world looks the same. All the girls are the same, too."

"I think this one's different," I said.

"I'll bet you fuck her."

"Maybe. You think it'll be the same at Da Nang?"

"Like Paris and Singapore?"

"Yeah."

The new girl came and put two beers on the bar. Pete paid her. "Look," she said, "I got this girlfriend. And I'm new here. And I told her if I met a coupla nice fellows who'd like to dance, maybe I'd see if we could go into town dancing later, after I get off. And y'all look harmless enough."

Before Pete or I could say anything she said, "I'm Janie Blue. We get together on Sunday nights and we go dancing. I'm working till nine. We're two fellows short."

We told her we would go and she went back to work. Other fliers were coming in for beer and whiskey. We went to the BOQ and put on clean cowboy shirts and deodorant and washed our faces. While we were tucking in our shirttails Pete said, "You know, this is the best part—knowing you're going to get it. The really best part is right before you put it in, when you're hovering over her. I always stop to smile right before I put it in. It's like when you're solo, sitting on the runway. You're looking down the nose of your bird pointing down the pavement and the tower tells you you're cleared, and you cob the power and pop the brakes, and all your gauges are good."

We walked fast, taking a shortcut through some woods on a sandy walk, in the dark, back to the bar at the club. At the bar we drank beer while we watched the girl we were going to dance with.

The operations staff duty officer came to the bar with the flight schedule for the week and gave us all copies.

"We'll both be up there alone, at the same time," I told Pete after we studied the schedule.

"Let's make up some bomb runs in case we get to go to war together."

"High dive. That's all I want to do," I said.

"We'll pick a target, practice this week," Pete said. "Pick one of these little shithole towns around here."

"You stay low," I said, "do a two-seventy. Come in low on a forty-five-degree-off run-in. When I call off-safe from my high dive, you'll be in your run."

"I love that low-angle shit. Man, I could run low-angle forever."

"Call it the scissors," I said.

"Pete and Truck scissors."

"Fucking A."

* * *

When Janie Blue got off work the three of us rode in her van to a lounge, me in the back lying flat and Pete in the passenger seat. The Tiki Lounge was decorated like a South Pacific place, palms, straw furniture, little fountains of water. The girls who worked there wore woven grass skirts, and the men's shirts were bright prints. The music was rock and roll and there was a big crowd. Beside the door where we went in was the tiki, a concrete statue, maybe two hundred pounds, shoulder high, that squatted with its arms out like it wanted to hold something. When Pete saw the tiki he picked it up, hugging it like it was a woman, and began to dance along with the slow song on the jukebox. He was able to dance gracefully with the tiki even when the songs got fast. Janie thought Pete was funny, dancing with the heavy statue, and when we got to her friends she pointed him out. Janie's friends were in a group by the bar on the other side of the dance floor; she took my hand and we walked around the edge. There were a lot of people dancing, but Pete and the tiki were the show. Janie introduced me as a guy from the base. It was too loud to hear names. The friends nodded their heads at Janie and smiled at me. There were two young men and three girls. The girl who was supposed to be with Pete was short, with dark skin and black, square-clipped bangs. She talked to Janie, then went to the bar and bought a beer and started drinking.

The room was all colors from the lights and the clothes—reds and greens, blues and yellows and the white light. The music was fast and hard. Most of the dancers had stopped and were standing around the edge of the dance floor, watching Pete dancing with the tiki. He moved like nobody was watching.

The bouncer went onto the dance floor and tapped him on the shoulder. Pete bowed, as if turning over his partner, but the bouncer, a big white man who wore tight clothes like a pirate, didn't laugh. He told Pete he would have to stop dancing with the tiki or leave, so Pete set the tiki in the middle of the dance floor. The fast rock and roll stopped. The bouncer took Pete by the arm, but Pete placed his hands on the man's cheeks and kissed the man on the tip of his nose. Everybody laughed and gave Pete an ovation, and the bouncer smiled as Pete walked away, leaving the tiki in the middle of the dance floor until the bouncer got someone to help him move the statue back beside the door.

Pete came to where Janie Blue and I were standing with the g. p. He was hot from dancing. Janie pointed to Pete's girl, who was drinking. Pete's girl moved closer to Pete. He put his arm around his girl and shouted, "Man! I love dancing!"

The room was opened to one side, to a deck. There was a breeze coming in from the deck, off the ocean. Somebody said we ought to go onto the deck. When we started moving, other groups started toward the deck too. Then somebody said we should go swimming. Pete's girl said she didn't have a bathing suit, and Pete said it didn't matter, so we all worked through the people at the edge of the dance floor and left the Tiki Lounge.

We got into Janie Blue's van and she drove several miles on an isolated road with us in the back of the van trying to remember lyrics to songs. We turned onto some hard sand and parked. We were near the shallows of the estuary. Most of the shore was muck and grass clumps, but we were on a spit of hard-packed sand. Two of the girls jumped out the back of the van ahead of me, and by the time I was out they had their blouses off and their hands behind their backs unfastening their bras. The two men were dancing in the sand, trying to get their pants off. I waited for Janie Blue to come from the driver's side and we took our clothes off too. The sand stuck to our bare skin. We watched each other while we smiled, then ran and jumped into the shallow water where the others were splashing and shouting and talking. I held Janie's hand while we crouched down so only our heads stuck out of the water. There was enough light from the city, reflecting off low clouds, to see the lines of trees and water and the dark shapes of the girls and the men; but the faces were shadows, even when they were close, especially the eyes.

Janie Blue and I were holding hands, bobbing and smiling,

watching the others cavort, when Pete called to me, "Look what I got, Truck! Come here!" Janie Blue and I waddled on our knees on the mucky bottom in chest-deep water toward the shadow of Pete and his girl. He was cradling her in his arms, on top of the water, and she had an arm around his neck. She was darker than the others with her dark skin. She had one breast out of the water, against Pete's chest. One breast floated where the waves and turbulence in the water caused it to be covered and uncovered. "Lighty tits!" Pete brought his hand from under the girl and sloshed water on her breast in the surface of the water, and it shone in a dim, green glow. "Irifuckindescent algae! This stuff in the water makes tits light up if you rub 'em! My girl's got lighty tits! I am a wealthy person!" He and the girl were giggling.

Janie Blue and I waddled on our knees toward the bank where the van was parked and sat with our bodies buoyed in the shallows and watched Pete and his girl and the other two couples have chicken fights. The naked girls would get on the men's shoulders and the couples would confront each other, and the girls would try to push each other off. Pete and his girl were winning most of the fights. When they beat one couple by knocking them over in the water, in a furious water fight, Pete lifted his girl straight over his head, off his shoulders, and turned his head around as far as he could and kissed her on the pussy. They both laughed, and Pete shouted, "I am a very wealthy man!"

In the morning there were some new guys in the cafeteria line waiting for Maria. Their flight suits were new and wrinkled, ill-fitting. Their patches were bright; they had just been sewn on—some patches had threads dangling from them. Maria was carrying on with her usual banter. Pete and I waited at the back of the line.

"Well, did you fuck her?"

"She's a nice girl, man."

Maria saw us and called, "Look who's here!" and the new guys looked at us, at our seasoned patches and our flight suits that were faded and form-fitting. Maria held her spatula in her left hand and did all the other work with her right, throwing sausage patties and bacon on the grill, cracking eggs. I had heard Maria say the same thing when I was a new guy and other old guys were in the back of the line. When Maria looked at us, all the new guys in line looked at us. They all looked pale. Those new guys who could not see well craned their necks down the line, their shaved heads in a row.

Pete walked past the new guys. They ducked back in line as he passed. He went to the front of the line and walked around the end of the counter and reached above the stainless-steel exhaust fan and switched the radio on. Maria eyeballed him and shook the spatula like she would hit him, her right hand on her hip, and Pete walked back around the front of the counter and past the new guys, who whispered to each other as they watched him pass.

The Gomez Funeral Parlor commercial was playing on the radio.

"Quiet!" Maria said.

The announcer said, "Welcome to the Obituary of the Air." The tinny electric organ played a hymn everybody knew. Then the man said, "Jesus Rodriguez, sixty-four, of two-fifteen Rio Verde Avenue, died early this morning. He is survived by his wife, Maria, and seven children." And he named the children.

BOOK TWO

THE WAR

OKINAWA–VIETNAM
APRIL–MAY 1970

I took a MAC flight to Okinawa. They called what happened there "staging." As soon as the MAC flight landed there was a briefing in an auditorium near the hangars. The briefing officer was a major. His words echoed in the auditorium. Officers and enlisted men would be segregated in Quonset huts. We would eat in separate lines in the same chow hall. They gave us lists of things we had to do in staging. It was up to us to do the things. They said it should take three days to get everything done: medicals, dentals, secret briefings, indoctrination sessions, confirmation on the manifest. Once we got on the manifest we knew which flight was ours, one of the two every day that shuttled between staging and in-country.

We had to get our gear, the stuff we would need in-country, and our issue was determined by what we would be doing once we got to the war. The supply building was a World War II airplane hangar converted into a warehouse. The building was metal with huge doors that rolled open on steel tracks in the concrete tarmac. A counter stretched across the space inside the open doors. Corporals and sergeants manned the counter. They wore jungle utilities, and they were smoking cigars and calling names. The sergeants talked more than the corporals. They made jokes about where the men getting the gear were going while they dispensed jungle utilities and jungle boots and jungle survival gear.

The other men waiting for their gear wore stateside uniforms, wrinkled from traveling, like mine, soaked from sweat on the muggy island. While they waited they smoked cigarettes and talked, leaning against the giant metal beams that supported the hangar. Some of the men laughed as they talked. Behind the counter, beyond the corporals and sergeants, were wooden bins full of high-use small stuff like hats and boots and belts and underwear. Behind the bins were rows of shelves that went halfway to the ceiling in the hangar, and leaning on the tops of the high shelves were ladders for the corporals and sergeants to climb to get the low-use items like communicators' headsets and tankers' helmets and gloves for the MPs.

We moved forward as each man drew his issue. The enlisted men in stateside uniforms like mine shuffled around, not in a line, and reassessed their position in the order every time it changed until everybody seemed comfortable with who was next and who was going to be served by which corporal or sergeant. I moved with them, blending in; then they settled back to their smoking and talking, not looking at each other, watching me because I was an officer, listening to the corporals and sergeants shouting names and asking for sizes.

When my turn came, I gave the sergeant my papers and he asked my specialty.

"Sixty-five-oh-one, A4E pilot," I told him.

"They lost one of your birds this morning—you know that, sir?"

"No."

"Heard it on the Armed Forces Radio News Network. You might have known the pilot. News comes on every thirty minutes. The gunny, out in the office—he cuts it on the loudspeakers, every thirty minutes. Wants us all to keep up with the latest from the war. Says it's our war, ought to keep up with it. The pilot got killed. You

gotta have a long flight suit? I'm short on longs. Reckon you can
get by with a regular, sir?"

"Regulars squeeze my nuts, " I said.

The sergeant took my paperwork and walked toward the bins
and aisles and turned into the maze. There was another counter
on the other side of the stored gear, at the other end of the aisles,
on the other side of the hangar, facing the other way. There were
no people on the other side, only the empty counter and closed
sliding doors.

When the sergeant came back with my gear I asked him, "You
ever open up that other side, like when you got a lot of people
waiting?" I motioned toward the enlisted men who were lounging
and watching us talk.

"It's open, Lieutenant." He was holding a rope, pulling a
wheeled hamper full of my new flight gear. "See, the idea is to take
this shit I got for you here in this bucket"—he pointed to the
hamper, dropping the rope—"and if you're still living a year from
now, you come through that side over there and give us our shit
back. Because this is not yours, Lieutenant; it belongs to the
taxpayers of our country, and you've got to promise to bring it back,
sir."

I checked my gear against the paperwork, stepping aside. The
sergeant called the next man. I put my gear in the new flight bag
that was on the list. A man in an operations jeep came with the
manifest, and everybody crowded around the jeep when it stopped
near the big sliding door.

I would be on the morning flight of May fourth. That meant I
would not get combat pay for April, because you had to originate
your flight that would terminate in Vietnam by midnight of the last
day of the month in order to get combat pay for that month.

I knew Pete was in the pipeline ahead of me. I knew he was already
at Da Nang, probably flying his ass off. I kept hoping when he got
there they had put him in some shit job, like base laundry officer

or communications specialist. I thought maybe he had been rerouted, maybe to a school, like sea survival or jungle survival. But I kept picturing him flying combat missions, getting ahead of me.

Each day of the five days I had to wait on Okinawa I went to base operations every morning to find the name of the pilot who had been killed. The clerks at base operations showed me all the messages, but there was no message on the pilot who had been killed. After going to base operations I went to my medical or dental or briefing, then back to my room in a Quonset hut and drank a bottle of Jack Daniel's. Every night I went to the chow hall drunk and ate all I could. The food was good. Then I went back to the Quonset hut each evening and passed out in the rack.

On the fifth day, on the C-130, I was smelling bad after five days of drinking. The other men on the plane were the same. We sat with our gear in webbing hung from the ceiling. There were no side windows in the rear of the airplane. We could see out a window up high near the front. We had to lean forward to see the window. The green hills of Okinawa were still; then they moved and went to a green blur; then the airplane groaned as it tucked in its extended parts, and we saw blue sky as we climbed, leaning toward the rear of the airplane with the force of gravity; then the airplane banked and we saw the grey-and-green ocean and wind-blown whitecaps. Once we were established on the flight course all we saw was clouds in the distance and, later, the bright white light inside the clouds. We stayed in the bright white light of the clouds for four hours, with the engines droning. People were feeling sick because there were no side windows in the rear.

It was dusk when the airplane descended out of the clouds, and when it banked to turn we all strained from our seats in the netting and looked out the window up high near the front. Lumpy-looking mountains dropped into the clear black waters of the South China Sea. The harbor was natural, protected from the sea by several of the lumps. The mountains and the harbor looked like they were connect-the-dot lights. Airplanes with flashing red and green

lights were constantly in and out of the visible part of the sky as
our airplane banked and maneuvered for the landing. We all
leaned forward and strained to see. Illumination flares dangled
from little parachutes and lit up the countryside. The flares were
fired so the grunts living out in the bush could see who was about
to blow them away. That's what the loadmaster told us. He flew
into Da Nang three nights every week. He got extra pay for it. He
flew in at dusk and right back out, early, before the rocket attacks
started.

The enlisted men who had gotten off the C-130 with me were
waiting in a line with their sea bags beside them, and some of them
saluted when we passed in the jeep. Their new sea bags were full
and their new camouflaged utilities were deep greens and browns
and ill-fitting. The high-pitched jet engine that powered the
generators on the C-130 was running, but she was dark except for
the running lights. She was making a screeching noise. When we
drove behind her I had to cover my ears. The jeep driver started
talking about trucks but I couldn't hear what he was saying. We
went through a gate with no sentry, an opening in the tall wire
fence, and came to a narrow asphalt street in time to stop for the
six-by trucks. There were floodlights on top of every fence post.
The lights were focused on the asphalt road. The six-bys went past,
decelerating; their diesel smoke rolled over us with the wind as
each passed, one after the other, and our jeep shuddered in each
blast. The lights of the jeep cut into the rolling smoke. The trucks
stopped on the asphalt street and the drivers dropped the tailgates
and men came out. The men were surefooted getting out of the
trucks. There were no commands, only the noise of the diesel truck
engines and the C-130's whine and the men's feet and gear hitting
the asphalt street as the men got out of the trucks and walked
toward the tarmac where the C-130 was parked. The men moved
quietly once they got their gear straight. Their jungle utilities were
faded to pastels and rotting around rotten boots. They had written
words and drawn characters and designs on their shirts and hats

with Magic Markers and some of the men needed to shave. As they got out of the trucks they looked at me in the jeep waiting to pull onto the asphalt street. I nodded to some of the men as they walked past, to the ones who looked into my eyes. They all went toward the C-130 in a file. When they were past us the driver stretched to see around the six-bys and pulled onto the asphalt street. "What's that smell, besides the diesel?" I shouted to him.

He wound the engine in each gear. His utilities were faded and clean and he was squared away, very military. The jeep jerked when he shifted. "The enlisted men shit in buckets," he said, "halves of fifty-five-gallon drums. Every morning the men on the shit detail go around and burn the buckets. They pour diesel fuel in and set the whole mess on fire. The only flush shitters are in the chow hall and the officers' head." He shouted. The enlisted men who got off the C-130 were getting on the trucks. They struggled with their heavy sea bags and clothes bags, climbing awkwardly into the backs of the six-bys as we drove past. The driver drove the jeep like it was a race car.

The asphalt street was narrow and the shoulders were sand. On the side of the road away from the runways was a fence, thick-meshed and rolled with barbed wire on top and on one side. At every fourth fence post was a light pole with a set of spotlights on top, like the lights at a small high school football field, and at the base of every other light was a sandbagged bunker with a machine gunner, a grenade launcher, and a radio operator crouched inside, looking away from the asphalt street, across an open ditch full of shit. On the other side of the ditch was an unpaved road, and on the other side of that road were the cardboard and scrap lumber shacks where the gooks lived. The shacks were made of crates and boxes with "Rice Krispies" and "Hamm's Beer" and federal stock numbers printed in faded ink across what had become walls and roofs and doors.

The driver said, "Sir, you'll have to find you a good gook to wash your stuff for you while you're here."

"How do you get a good one?"

"You can sign up for one. They call 'em mama-sans. That gate right there is where they strip-search the gook women when they come in the morning to work." He pointed to a guarded entrance to a bridge across the shit ditch. In the entrance were little wooden cubicles. "Then they search 'em again when they go home at night. They all look the same."

"How do you tell a good one from a bad one?"

"I guess if they're on the other side they're bad gooks, sir."

"Other side of what?"

"The shit ditch."

The gooks lived inside the cardboard shacks. Some were cooking over open fires, and some were walking along the unpaved road and among the shacks. Some of the gooks were riding bicycles with gaudy pieces of metal and plastic decorating them. Some of the gooks, very few, rode motorbikes on the road and commandeered their routes from the walkers and bicyclists, blowing their electric horns and shouting as they wound along the unpaved road. Gook men in shorts and undershirts had their asses draped across the edge of the ditch, shitting. Women stopped and pulled their pajama pants down and put their wrists next to their crotches, and when they pissed the liquid ran down their wrists and off their two extended fingers, like a fake dick; and when they finished pissing they wiped their fingers and wrists on their long, loose britches, on the flares near the ground; then they pulled their britches up and continued to walk along the unpaved road past the men shitting in the ditch. The marines in the sandbagged bunkers watched the gooks in the light from the floods. Some of the women who were walking had poles across their backs with a bucket hanging from each end of the poles. They chattered while they walked.

The driver asked me if I knew the pilot who was killed earlier in the week. I told him I didn't know who the pilot was, but if I knew his name I might remember him from flight school. The driver turned off the asphalt road, toward the runways. We went through a gate with no sentry into the MAG-11 living compound.

Quonset huts were in rows, each with a painted official sign in front with "Lt.——" or "Capt.——" stenciled in gold on a red background. In the center of the rows of Quonset huts was the MAG-11 officers' club. There was a sign, painted plywood, a group insignia, Gothic lions with airplanes in their raised paws. The parking lot was empty. The whole compound was lit by floodlights on poles. The driver stopped in the parking lot. I got out of the jeep and lifted my flight bag out. He left, throwing gravel.

The officers' club was made of scrap lumber that had weathered in the climate. The sign over the door said THE FINEST AIRPLANE DRIVERS IN THE WORLD ENTER HERE. The rafters were exposed. They were trusses hand made of scrap lumber. The walls and floor were plywood, and on the walls were photographs of the squadrons and the group and the changes of command. Beer labels were stuck to the bare wood between the pictures on the walls. Small wood tables had metal folding chairs around them, and the bar, along one wall, was for standing.

The bartender was the only person in the bar. He was thin, wiry, with thick glasses and a hook nose. He chewed gum. The bartender said I was the first new pilot to come through in a long time, but they would need me because they had just lost a pilot. He told me the pilot who had died was named Captain Reed, and he was the one who had broken the rafter in the middle of the room, causing the bow in the ridge of the roof. It had happened one night when all the A4E drivers got drunk and were climbing into the rafters and hanging by their legs and arms, singing. The group commander ordered that anyone climbing into the rafters would have to buy everybody in the bar a drink, with a minimum of a hundred dollars, and Captain Reed had thrown his hundred-dollar bill at the group commander and stayed in the rafters until there was a loud crack and the ridge of the roof bowed. Captain Reed was killed the next night diving on some guns.

The bartender told me the club had been a temporary chow hall for feeding all the airplane people, but when headquarters realized we were all going to be there for a long time they built a permanent chow hall and the officers took the old one for their club. At first the floor was discarded matting that had been the runway at Da Nang, but the officers of MAG-11 had saved and salvaged enough scrap plywood to cover the discarded metal matting. The plywood was stained with spilt beer and whiskey and wine and cigarette burns.

The bartender served cans of Hamm's beer or Jack Daniel's or wine by the case. The wine was usually for special occasions, like somebody going home or getting a hundred missions. The bartender said all the officers were at the new chow hall, at a banquet to honor Captain Reed. Then he asked me if I was going to stick around for the Kent State party. He said Kent State was a college somewhere in the Midwest and soldiers had been sent there and had shot some draft-dodging queers, and when everybody finished at the banquet they were going to celebrate the killing of the queers and have a big Kent State party. He had ordered an extra forty cases of wine.

The airplane drivers drifted in, laughing as they came through the swinging wooden doors. The A4E drivers wore red party suits, silk flight suits. Each one looked at the clock, then at me, then toward a table or the bar. Pete was the first to arrive at the bar, and he stopped in front of me.

"Suit, flying, silk, handmade, party, one each, red. Got a blow job from a gook bitch while her husband made it for me. Welcome to the war."

"It was the luck of the draw," I said.

"I get to fuck the lady," Pete said. "I saw her first."

The bartender brought a bottle of Jack Daniel's and a jar of water. Pete asked him, "Gunny Joe! You meet my friend Truck?"

"Yes sir, we've been chatting, sir."

"Truck Hardy, this is Gunny Joe. The gunny briefs us every day at sixteen hundred hours, tells us where our targets will be. Then he comes here and opens the bar, while we fly, and after we fly we come back here and Gunny Joe feeds us whiskey."

I said, "Tell me about Captain Reed."

Pete said, "Yeah. We just had a thing for him over at the chow hall."

"You don't have to come to the briefing every day unless you're on the schedule, sir," Gunny Joe said. "Some of the new pilots like to come every day for a while just to get to know the usual target areas, so when you start flying over there you'll know enough about the area to find the targets. I'll help you get snapped in, sir."

Pilots in red party suits were seated at the tables, on the metal folding chairs, while pilots in navy-blue and royal-blue party suits—the F4B and A6A drivers—were coming in one at a time or in small groups. Several of the men had one-hundred-mission patches sewn on their sleeves. All the men were smiling as they came into the club talking, looking for places to sit or stand; most had mustaches and shaved heads. They all glanced at the wall behind the bar when they entered. The clock on the wall was octagonal, outlined by white neon, with lighted red numbers on a gold background, and lighted green hands. "Should take six months," Pete said. His hair was in a crew cut. "There's no reason why you can't get a hundred missions in six months. I've already got twelve."

The men at the tables and the ones walking in were shouting, "Gunny Joe! The finest airplane drivers in the world need wine!" and "How about some word on the shooting of the queers!"

"Welcome aboard, sir. I'll speak with you later about the briefings," Gunny Joe said, and he backed away and went to his cooler, then took a case of wine to a table.

Pete said, "Went across the border last night. That antiaircraft fire is some hot shit. It's like fucking for hours without stopping."

"Did you kiss somebody's ass to get here first?"

"They take the hottest stick men first."

"Tell me the truth," I said.

"I went up to wing after I got here and asked when you were coming. They said I was the last one on the April quota and you were the first one on the May quota. The alphabet got you, Hardy. I saw the lady first, so I get to fuck the lady."

"We'll see who fucks the lady," I said.

"The birds are in good shape," Pete said. "You never cancel for a broken airplane. You destroy the target with what you've got." He looked at the clock, then toward the door, and said, "Wait one." Pete walked over to meet a lieutenant colonel who spoke to Pete then looked at me. They walked toward me and I straightened myself at the bar. As they got to the bar Pete said, "This is Truck Hardy, sir. This is John Rossi."

The lieutenant colonel said, "I hear you're a natural." His head was shaved, he was stocky in his flight suit—a Borgnine little fellow with heavy brows. The butt of a cigar was between his teeth on the left side of his mouth.

"I like to fly, sir."

We shook hands.

"Welcome aboard, Hardy."

"Thank you, sir."

"I'm going over here and drink some wine. You be in my office at zero eight hundred and we'll take a little ride."

"I'll be ready, sir."

John Rossi walked away, toward a table where some majors in red party suits were rolling dice. He spoke to a lieutenant colonel in a navy-blue party suit, leaning over to say something, making a motion with his hand, a thumbs-up.

Pete said, "He'll take you dive-bombing on a hard target. Probably won't get shot at." Pete poured Jack Daniel's in my glass and his glass, then added water to each. I took my drink and he took his and he said, "Here's to no tomorrow," and we drank. "Once he knows you can hit the target, he'll stick you in the midst of the fray. We're going to fly every day. And I get two hundred first."

"I bet a case of Jack Daniel's I get two hundred missions before you do," I said.

Pete poured Jack Daniel's in my glass and his glass, then added water to each. I took my drink and he took his and he said, "Two hundred." We drank.

"Tell me what happened to Captain Reed," I said.

Pete said, "He had two hundred missions. He was diving on guns at night."

As more pilots came into the club, more stood at the bar. Pete and I had to draw our whiskey and water and glasses closer, and we huddled together.

I asked him, "You dived on guns at night yet?"

"No. They don't let you do that for a long time. The night before Captain Reed went in he climbed up in the rafters and one of them broke."

"Gunny Joe showed me," I said. We turned toward the crowded room and looked at the clock, then up at the rafters, at the place where one was broken. All the pilots in the air group were in the club, packed around the tables and the bar. They were talking, laughing, drinking wine, moving their hands like little airplanes; they were in groups of red, royal-blue and navy-blue party suits.

"Gunny Joe tell you about the pissing contest?" Pete asked.

"No." We turned back toward the bar and drank some more Jack Daniel's. The pilots were talking louder, crowded around the tables, and some were smoking. As the room got hot, the smell of stale beer and wine and whiskey came out of the wood.

Pete said, "The night the rafter broke, Captain Reed was in here talking about killing gooks. He told us about a hop he flew last week, a daytime close-air-support scramble. They caught a couple of hundred gooks in the open and went in on a ten-degree dive with snakes. Had daisy-cutter fusing. They killed all the gooks, and Captain Reed said he made his victory pass, rolled inverted carrying five-fifty, and he said he looked through the canopy, still inverted, and all he could see was dead gooks. Said it was the greatest hop he'd ever flown.

"Then he got to drinking heavy, drinking Jack Daniel's, and after a while he had to pee, so he went outside, and there was this warrant officer out there, Ronnie Myers, ordnance officer, and

Ronnie was pissing over the top of a Quonset hut, where they keep the supplies for the laundry. So Captain Reed says, 'Can you do that again?' and Ronnie Myers says, 'I always piss like this when I drink beer.' So Captain Reed brings him back into the club and buys Ronnie Myers a case of Hamm's and tells Ronnie Myers to drink it fast, and Captain Reed disappears and Ronnie Myers sits there and works on the case of beer."

Gunny Joe finished serving wine to the tables and the other parts of the bar and came to where Pete and I were talking. He said, "Lieutenant Hardy, the Tomcat commander told me you're supposed to be some kind of hot shit."

"Pete's been telling everybody that just to give me a case of the ass for my fam hop with the skipper. Pete's the flyboy. Don't you and your intelligence boys know he's got the hot hands? How soon do we get to go up together?"

Pete said, "I can make section leader in a month."

Gunny Joe said, "If you're over-the-fence qual by then you can fly on his wing, except for night dive-bombing on guns. You have to get checked out by the Tomcat commander before you can dive-bomb on guns at night."

I asked, "How long before we can both fly at the same time?"

Pete said, "You want to play?"

I said, "Never let it be said that Truck Hardy was ever not ready to play."

Gunny Joe gave us a fresh bottle of Jack Daniel's and clean glasses. "Tomcat commander will snap you in tomorrow morning. Come to the sixteen-hundred-hours brief, sir." Gunny Joe walked toward his cooler.

We huddled at the bar. Pete said, "Ronnie Myers was sitting right over there drinking this case of beer. Everybody started talking about the tactics and strategy of pissing over a Quonset hut. We kept a fresh beer in front of Ronnie Myers all the time." Pete poured us some Jack Daniel's. "We let him piss once, and we watched his style but refused to let him go for distance. After about maybe an hour we all went outside, and here comes Captain Reed in Colonel Rossi's jeep leading a convoy of a hundred Air Force crewmen, F4C drivers from the Wolfpack group, the Air Force pukes from the other side of the runway. And these Air Force crewmen had on their flight suits and patches and scarves and mustaches, and there were twenty Navy people, and fifty Army officers, all drunk in their utilities. Jeeps, trucks, motorcycles all pulled into the parking lot behind the club. The Quonset hut where they keep the supplies for the laundry was roped off. A platoon of Marine infantry set up their machine guns and grenade launchers to protect the site from sappers. A helicopter circled overhead. The colonel from the Wolfpack group got out of a jeep and walked to the passenger side. Their man unfolded out of the jeep. Bronski was huge, with big hands, a big neck, and heavy brows, flight-suit sleeves rolled up, tremendous arms. He was drunk. The Wolfpack commander and Tomcat commander shook hands and talked. The men in the crowd were straining to see, making side bets, drinking Jack Daniel's and Hamm's. A flight of Phantoms went overhead at two hundred feet, afterburners blowing full bore. Nobody looked up. The Wolfpack commander and Tomcat commander led Bronski and Ronnie Myers to the side of the Quonset hut and signaled for silence. Myers and Bronski shook hands and talked for a minute, and all the time these two hundred airplane drivers and some ground pounders are closing in around the hut, trying to see. The Wolfpack commander said, 'Gentlemen, the basis of the wager is that Mister Myers will clear the hut and Lieutenant Bronski will not. If there is any other result, Lieutenant Bronski will be the winner.'

"So the two commanders step off three paces, even their marks, and draw a line in the sand. Bronski and Myers toed the line. The crowd got noisy. Tomcat commander fired a red tracer, a thirty-eight round. The helicopter came screaming in, machine guns hanging out both sides. Some private out on the perimeter got excited and started shooting his machine gun and killed a gook who was sitting across the ditch shitting. Everybody was shouting and cheering and kibitzing, and Bronski started pissing right away, slowly climbing the sides of the Quonset hut. He was leaning forward slightly, his body was tight. Ronnie just stood still and fumbled with his trousers for a minute, weaving back and forth real slow. Ronnie stood still, then his face tightened, and Captain Reed hollered, 'Don't strain, Ronnie!' Bronski was half-way to the crest of the building, with good velocities, and Ronnie Myers started with a rush, and as soon as he hit the side of the Quonset hut his bowels broke—he pissed on his boots and slumped down to the ground, passed out cold. Then Bronski lost his concentration and finished in a puddle in the sand."

"How much did you lose?"

"Five hundred. They said Captain Reed lost about ten grand."

"No shit?"

"The next night he got blown away."

We both looked at the clock.

"You reckon I'll get blown away?"

"You ain't going to die here, Hardy. You're going to get shot fucking some married woman."

"I don't fuck married women."

"You'll learn how."

We looked at the clock.

"If I do get blown away I want you to do me a favor. There's a little piece of land at home called the Hainted Place. It's real pretty. There's a dirt road that goes right down the middle of it, and the road's straight as an arrow for two miles. Get them to have a ceremony in the pasture down in the bottomland next to the dirt road where it crosses the creek, and while everybody who cares enough to come is gathered there you bring a flight of twelve birds through there, down that straight dirt road, hauling ass, balls to the wall, right in the treetops; and when you get right over the top of those who are gathered there you let everybody else keep going level and you pull your nose up and go straight up until you're out of sight and there's no more rumble. Have some-body on the ground tell those people that I never did like to operate in the horizontal. Say I was a vertical man, a solo vertical man."

"You're not going to get blasted."

"Just say you will."

"Fucking A."

All the pilots who weren't flying went to the club at fifteen hundred hours. We slipped into the cool, dark, empty bar and mixed
our own drinks; then the pilots scheduled to fly in the next
twenty-four hours went to shuttle stop number ten, the officers'
club, at fifteen forty-five to catch the six-by. The six-by ran a
continuous shuttle from the living area to the flight line along the
narrow asphalt road, by the fence and the floodlights and the shit
ditch, parallel to the runways, in a fifteen-minute cycle. A ladder
was hung on the tailgate of the six-by, and when a six-by blew past
every fifteen minutes, with its hot diesel smoke and red dust, and
stopped, the load of men inside stood and filed off, coming
backwards down the ladder. The pilots at shuttle stop number ten,
the officers' club, waited until the incoming men were off the
six-by, then they mounted the ladder according to rank. Any
enlisted men who needed a ride to the flight line got on, if they
could, after the pilots, or they waited for the sixteen-hundred
shuttle. The gooks on the other side of the shit ditch kept walking
or cycling or feeding their pigs or shitting, but they watched and
counted the pilots who got on the six-by, distinguishing pilots from
enlisted men by the shoulder-holstered pistols versus the M-16
rifles. The pilots who would not be flying were in the club mixing
their own martinis, waiting for Gunny Joe to finish the
sixteen-hundred-hours brief so he could catch the six-by to the
club and start serving drinks.

The six-by drivers were shitbirds, enlisted men who were
always screwing up. Driving the shuttle was the worst punish-
ment in MAG-11. Only the men who were busted to private for
drinking or whoring or cussing the NCOs were sent to the motor
pool to do time driving the shuttle; they all drove the same way,
double clutching, grabbing gears, either accelerating or slamming
the air brakes. We held on the best we could but slid forward or

backward on the wooden benches along the sides in the back of the six-by. The drivers were required by regulations to come to a full stop at each shuttle stop and call the number and name of the stop loud enough for the passengers in the back to hear. The operations bunker where Gunny Joe gave the sixteen-hundred-hours brief was stop number one, and the officers' club was stop number ten.

The shitbird driver would shout, "Number nine! Chow hall!" and the pilots on the shuttle would shout, "Number nine, chow hall!" All the way down the asphalt road we would shout the right number at the right stop. The gooks on the other side of the shit ditch would wave when the passengers shouted at the stops, and the gooks always smiled when they waved. Except for shouting the name of each stop, the pilots did not talk while we were riding on the six-by, but sometimes the shitbird driver would shout back at us, in between stops, while he was jamming gears and we were hanging on: "Sir! What do you fuckers do when you fly them airplanes over there, sir? You kill gooks? How many gooks do you kill every night, sir? I'd love to go over there and kill a bunch of gooks."

Stop number one, the operations bunker, was a hole in the ground with a sand roof, head high, and sandbag walls. The enlisted men who did the intelligence work lay in the sun in their lounge chairs on the clear sand on the level roof. Outside the sandbag walls, off the edge of the roof, were metal barrels full of sand, all the way around the bunker. Along with the maze of antennas there were always enlisted men in the lounge chairs on the roof at sixteen hundred hours in their jocks and aviator sunglasses, and when the six-by screamed to a halt and the pilots shouted, "Number one, operations bunker!" the enlisted men in the lounge chairs on the roof sat up and watched. They were the intelligence off shift. They were the intelligence on shift when we landed in the middle of the night, coming back from our missions, and they took our debriefs. We told them what we had done. When we got off the six-by, climbing backwards down the ladder, the enlisted men in the intelligence off shift made book on us. "Ten bucks says magnet-ass Hardy takes two hundred rounds tonight on mission number six-seven-three-niner" or "I'm taking Major Davis to show." They always talked loud and laughed loud to each other. They would glance down on us from the roof of the bunker as we walked on the wooden catwalk from the six-by and went down the wooden steps into the bunker. Some of the pilots would look up at the enlisted men in the intelligence off shift and smile, but most of us looked into the dark hole where the wooden steps went and our eyes would adjust to the dark. Once we got to the bottom of the steps there was a short tunnel lit by dim bulbs. At the end of the dim tunnel was a closed door that led to the large, bright briefing room.

IN-COUNTRY
JANUARY–APRIL 1971

I spent nine months in-country. It was my two hundred and eighteenth mission, a night dive-bombing hop on the Ho Chi Minh Trail, when Colonel Laughlin got blown away. I was flying on his wing. Colonel Laughlin had been in the squadron about a month, fresh from a tour as air attaché to the American ambassador to India. I saw him get hit. He was in his second dive. There was an explosion in the air, where he would have been; then everything was dark again; then a glimmer, then a glow appeared. In the dive his airplane became brighter until the impact. I called Moonbeam on guard and told them to launch the rescue. I hung around where Colonel Laughlin went in as long as I could, above thirteen thousand feet, out of range of the eighty-fives, driving around in circles, talking to Moonbeam about how to set up the rescue, watching the night jungle for dim flickers of lights to appear here and there. The beginning of a rescue meant the end of the bombing, and the gooks would drive their trucks on the trail with their lights on, carrying supplies and ammunition south without worrying about getting bombed. My fuel got low. I never heard Colonel Laughlin's rescue beacon on guard, and I never heard him call on guard using the radio in his survival pack. I went back to Da Nang and filed my debrief.

Gunny Joe stood in the front of the briefing room, pointer in hand. "Lieutenant Hardy took fire from two guns, located here . . . and here. He never saw any radar warning lights." Gunny Joe pointed to spots on the wall-sized map. "When Colonel Laughlin rolled in, eighty-five-millimeter guns tracked him. CJ-1 went in at first light and took pictures. The seat is still in the air frame. Colonel Laughlin took a direct hit—possibly two." Gunny Joe took a step and hit two wall switches, dimming the lights and turning on a slide projector. A black-and-white photograph image appeared on the front wall, a dirt road winding between mountains, bomb craters and broken, twisted trees.

"The object here"—he put the pointer on a small, dark spot—"is a Russian-made field generator. We believe its purpose is to power a radar tracking system, and that Colonel Laughlin was locked by radar. The radar site is probably on this ridge, less than two hundred meters from the border." He hit the switches again and dropped the pointer from the wall, holding it in both hands as the lights came on.

Colonel Rossi got up from his chair next to the side wall. "Thank you, Gunny." He walked to the middle of the room, in front of the map, watching the red and gold linoleum squares pass under him, a chewed cigar in his hand. His green Nomex flight suit sagged at the wrists and ankles but was tight everywhere else. "Colonel Laughlin's memorial service is at fourteen hundred hours tomorrow up at wing. Wear your party suits." He stopped and faced us.

"Gentlemen, the gooks have moved all their stuff down the trail from outside Vinh because of the bombing halt. Fifth Air Force ordered a B-52 strike, and Washington told them they can't have it because it's close to the border. We asked for this mission, and the Air Force is giving us one crack at it."

He put the cigar in his mouth and chewed, then pushed up the sleeves on his flight suit. "Hardy!"

"Sir!"

Colonel Rossi looked toward the wall-size map. He took the cigar out of his mouth and said, "Pick your wingman."

I looked around the room at the other men sitting in straight chairs. Most were stone-faced, looking straight ahead. Some were making notes on their knee-pad briefing cards.

"Pete, sir."

"Why?"

"We went to flight school together, sir."

Colonel Rossi looked at his S-3 officer, who nodded.

"Okay. . . . Gentlemen, the only way to hit the ridge is with a run-in heading of zero three eight. I'll come from the north, over the mountain, in ten-degree dives and *make* them shoot. They'll be cranked down when you roll in, so their guns will have to make big sector changes to pick you up, and the kind of radar they got doesn't move fast. You've got to boresight those bastards, high-dive, as steep as you can get. Even if you pickle high, you'll cross the border on your pullout. If you get shot, don't land up north. You and your airplane have got to end up somewhere inside the right country. But get the fucking guns."

The flight equipment of the crews hung still in little cubicles on all four walls of the ready room. We put on all our gear—torso harness, speed jeans, Nomex gloves—and we laid our survival vests on the counter. *Thirty-eight revolver with tracer rounds. Canned, dehydrated food. Candy bars. Cans of water. First-aid and sewing pouches. Survival knife. UHF radio. Silk scarf* with directions printed in six Oriental languages instructing the holder to help this downed American airman reach safety and explaining that the silk scarf was redeemable by any holder at any American consulate for ten thousand American dollars in gold. We called the scarf our blood chit.

We packed the objects in our survival vests and slung the vests around our arms and picked up the helmet bags and walked through the hangar out to the dark, past the diesel generators and an airplane turning up on the test pad; to the night heat, to the lit revetments where the airplanes sat like bug-eyed crabs looking out of their holes, all in a row. Past the revetments were the blue and yellow lights on the taxiway and runway. Auxiliary power units were screeching, pumping power into the airplanes. The rotating beacons were turning. The position lights were on. We hunkered in our flight gear and watched the ordnance crew fuse the bombs.

"Remember the ol' Pete and Truck scissors?" I asked Pete. "Remember that night we went up north of Mu Gia and hit a suspected bend in the river?"

"The night they had green tracers. That was a great night."

"How many rounds did we take that night? Three hundred? Four hundred?"

"A bunch."

"That was all thirty-sevens and fifty-sevens."

"Yeah. No eighty-fives."

"No eighty-fives."

"What if I boresight the bastards? Get 'em to shoot. You commence when I do, but come in shallow—catch 'em while they're up with me?"

"Nah. I want to boresight the bastards too. I want to feel it when it hits."

"Count fifteen when I call in, then commence. We go Winchester before we go target."

Winchester was thirty-thirty, the UHF frequency we used in flight school when we were both flying solo, assing around Texas, and we wanted to talk. We used "Winchester" because Winchester was what won the West.

I sat in the dark in my cockpit in the arming area while men pulled the ordnance pins and made the final checks. I held my hands above my helmet, fingers spread apart. My plane captain on the ground watched my hands and gave signals with his flashlights to his men working under my airplane. He could see I was not touching any switches or buttons or dials while his men armed my fuses. Pete's airplane rolled up off my starboard wing, moving like a mechanical toy, plodding and sucking and hissing, dark and lifeless. I returned my plane captain's salute and waited for Pete's lights to flash. They did.

"Da Nang ground: manual six-niner taxi for takeoff."

"Manual six-niner: taxi runway one-seven right; altimeter two niner-niner-four, temperature two-three, time one-seven-zero one and a half."

I advanced the throttle and turned the nose toward the taxiway. Pete clung to my wing like a shadow.

Trim is zero, zero, and six; flags are gone; flaps, slats, stabilizer; boards and hydraulics; fuel check; override good; seat armed, harness locked; controls are free; flapperons.

I entered the coordinates of targets, aim points, navigation points, and escape routes while I taxied, then switched the UHF. "Tower: manual six-niner, takeoff."

"Manual six-niner: taxi into position and hold, runway one-seven right."

"Hold on the right."

I aligned on the left half of the runway and stomped the brakes. Pete was there on the right, no lights. A cargo bird, dull black, crossed left to right halfway down the concrete strip; its lights cut slices through the mist, and its propellers sliced slivers of the blue and yellow lights. The headset in the helmet transmitted the UHF, guard, and ECM.

"Manual six-niner: cleared for takeoff runway one-seven right. Wind three three-zero degrees at two."

"Cleared on the right."

I advanced the throttle and looked in the mirror at Pete. His shadow's lights came on, red and green and pale yellow, outlining the harsh profile. The lights went off, leaving only the shadow.

RPM's up, EGT's coming; oil pressure; fuel flow; hydraulics; no lights; controls free; off at zero-three.

The airplane started slowly, heavy with fuel and bombs. *EGT up.* She started rolling. *Airspeed; good engine; angle of attack; oil, hydraulics, no lights; two thousand feet a hundred knots; three thousand feet a hundred and twenty; refusal.* The sound of the engine was a distant roar that changed pitch as the speed increased.

Pete said, "Rolling." I ate up seven thousand feet of runway and rotated, raised my gear, and went into the clouds four hundred feet off the ground.

Three up. Then over the UHF, "Switching." I heard a mike click twice. Pete was airborne. I changed the UHF frequency.

"Departure: manual six-niner is airborne to work with Moonbeam, one-eight-zero at four and a half passing one-two hundred for twenty-point-five, squawking two-three-two ident. Request outbound track on the two-five-zero-degree radial, your channel."

"Manual six-niner: radar contact. You're cleared as requested, sir."

I climbed through four thousand feet, still in the goo. There was a pause, a quiet except for the faint whine of the engines and the background hum of the headset. Then I busted through the tops of the clouds at eight thousand feet to a bright moon and a clear sky and climbed outbound from Da Nang. I saw Pete at five o'clock low, two miles behind, his shadow skimming the clouds, climbing for the rendezvous.

"Departure: manual six-niner is switching Moonbeam."

"Roger, sir. Have a good flight."

I switched the UHF. The dials tumbled and clicked into sync, and Pete clicked his mike to let me know he was up.

"Moonbeam: manual six-niner is airborne Da Nang with delta twos, delta charlie fusing, mission number six-seven-three-niner."

"Manual six-niner: Moonbeam. You are cleared to target area.

Come starboard to track outbound on the two-eight-zero-degree radial. Call departing."

Pete tucked tight under my port wing when I leveled. We rode quietly. Below was darkness, no clouds. There was an occasional firefight with streams of tracers going toward each other and bright bleeps and flashes when mortars and grenades went off. Sometimes the B-52's would come through and drop their tons of bombs in long strings that looked like a giant was running through the dark jungle stepping on firecrackers.

"Moonbeam: canasta zero-seven's a flight of four alpha sevens. We're off Yankee Station to work with you."

"Canasta zero-seven: your mission number is six-six-four-eight. You'll be working with Copperhead—repeat, Copperhead."

"Roger that. What's your question tonight?"

"Who was Yancey Derringer's sidekick?"

"Oh, shit. That's a toughie."

"Yes, sir. We've had seven customers miss it."

"Maybe one of my wingmen knows. Dash two?"

"Naw, but it was an Indian."

"Three?"

"No, sir."

"Four?"

"Negative."

"Moonbeam: canasta zero-seven does not know. Anybody else up this freq?"

"Sir, we have manual six-niner, a flight of Marine birds."

"Hey, six-niner: don't you know who Yancey Derringer's sidekick was? You marines are supposed to know shit like that."

"Pahoo," I said.

"That right, Moonbeam?"

"Yes, sir. Manual six-niner got it and owns the question."

We crossed the border into Laos and I said, "Who was Liz Taylor's third husband? Switching target."

"That's a good question. Have a good flight, sir."

I rocked my wings. We switched to Winchester.

"You there?" I asked.

"Yeah."

"How's your bird?"

"Tight."

"Go target."

Pete's mike clicked.

"Manual six-niner's up."

"Roger, six-niner: This is Copperhead. Hold on x-ray zulu. Stand by."

We banked in gentle turns. I anchored my downwind leg on the orbit point fifteen miles from the target. We were still high at twenty thousand feet. There were no lights on the ground. Pete clung to my wing. His bird was dark. We made our turns.

"Manual six-niner: Copperhead. You are cleared to the target. Manual zero-one actual is executing. Establish contact. You are cleared to execute."

I turned the formation light off and pulled back on the throttle, allowing the nose of the airplane to drop slightly, banking to the right, changing course by forty degrees while descending. Pete hung tight on my starboard wing.

Harness locked; lights out, good engine; bombs set, arming switch to go.

I rolled out of the turn and leveled at fifteen thousand feet. The twenty-threes and thirty-sevens on the mountains near our target began their barrage. Streaks of tracers, six to the clip, snaked in a low profile to our port, to the north.

Colonel Rossi came up on UHF. "Manual zero-one actual in hot."

"Six-niner's up. Tally," I said.

The eighty-fives started down low to the north. When the big guns fired, the bright blast on the ground lit the mountains and valleys and gave a strobe view of the same thing we had seen in the picture on the wall of the briefing room. The tracers were white and bigger and had red burning tails, and they went farther and burned brighter when they blew than the twenty-threes or thirty-sevens or even the fifty-sevens.

Pete's wings rocked and his engine roared as he separated himself from me. Then his Skyhawk descended, banked hard, and disappeared. I pulled the master armament switch out of its detent, lifted it over the hump, and locked it down, making my bird hot.

"Manual six-niner is in hot."

Colonel Rossi said, "Roger. Off cold."

The shooting toward the north stopped when I called in hot. My radar altimeter told me how far I was from the ground. I rolled to my port. Colonel Rossi's bombs started their string of flashes on the mountain. Thirteen thousand feet. The nose dropped and I steadied in a thirty-degree dive. They locked me up with radar. My ECM lights came on and the beeper sounded. I dumped chaff. I hit the concussion waves from the eighty-fives, then the waves from Colonel Rossi's bombs; then I steadied my pipper, a dot of light through the gunsight, on the spot where the guns had fired. I could still see the image of the guns firing, the bright blast in the night. The shooting started. At first it was small stuff in a barrage, twenty-threes and thirty-sevens in clips of six. The red tracers moved silently upward through the dark like ghosts and they burnt out after a while, between my airplane and the ground, before they got high enough; but when they went off they lit the sky in front of me, hundreds of them in groups of white flashes. They came from both sides and from the front. Then the eighty-fives came up. My dive was good, my pipper was on the guns. I counted altitude backwards; I was looking at them shooting at me, at the bright blasts. The big white tracers came one at a time, fast and cumbersome. When I reached drop altitude I pickled and my bombs released. The tracers were going over and under my wings, coming at my nose and missing me at the last instant.

"Off cold," I said.

Pete called, "In hot."

I pulled hard on the stick, as many Gs as I could, up and to starboard. Four more eighty-fives started in unison, tracking Pete in his dive. My ECM light went off and the beeper stopped. I released my Gs and stayed low and the airplane jolted upward, in a thunderous noise, compressing me in my seat. I grunted. There was smoke in the cockpit. The engine fire light came on. I pulled the throttle to idle and zoomed. A huge explosion lit the valley like daylight, stayed lit, then dimmed slowly until only a fire remained.

I switched the UHF to Winchester. "Say your position," I said. I watched the fire on the ground, where the guns had been.

As my airspeed bled I eased the throttle forward.

RPM coming; EGT seven two zero; hydraulics; fire light; smoke gone; come on, fire light. The fire light went out. I advanced the throttle and nursed the airplane higher, bringing on the power slowly and studying the gauges, and repeated, "Say your position."

The engine was rough. I was yawing to starboard from the induced drag of the new hole in my wing. The controls were positive, no slack. The fire was out. I came port to a heading of zero-nine-zero.

"If you read, acknowledge," I said. I made a visual check of the UHF.

I leveled at thirteen thousand feet and looked over my shoulder, turning as much as I could, as soon as I could, in the seat, trying to see the rear quadrant of the flight path. I drove straight and level and waited and looked back and forth between the inside and the dark. The fire on the ground was burning bright.

"If you read, acknowledge," I repeated.

"Manual six-niner: Moonbeam on guard. Come starboard to heading one-eight-zero." I switched the UHF to guard.

"Do you have a tally on my wingman?"

"Negative, manual six-niner. Come starboard to one-eight-zero."

"Moonbeam: manual six-niner is a prebriefed rendezvous."

"Come starboard heading one-eight-zero."

I turned and fire ripped into the cockpit from below. The heat burned through to my ass. Two more eighty-five-millimeter rounds went past to starboard. I grabbed the face curtain with both hands, palms toward my face, and pulled the curtain down in front of my face, and my seat blasted out of the airplane. My legs and arms flailed in the stream of cold air; my breathing was taken: then my parachute opened and I looked straight ahead and crossed my legs, tight, so I wouldn't bust my balls on a tree limb, and I grunted, like they taught us, and got my breath back. After the shock of the opening parachute I floated, breathing heavy. It was pure dark; my eyes were dulled by the bright blast of the ejection. There was no motion, no sound except the wind and my breathing. My airplane trailed fire for a while. I had zoomed, so the airplane kept flying up after I left it. Then the airplane rolled and the engine blew and the airplane tumbled and came apart in fire. I heard it crash way away. The wind I was falling through was warmer.

The trees below, in the distance, looked like trees back home from the air at night, until I felt the heat of the air. What appeared to be the ground, in the dim light, was really another layer, the tops of other trees. There were some grassy areas that were grey against the black of the layers of trees, and the grass was thick and deep. I held on to the risers of the parachute with my legs crossed until I landed with a thud in some grass taller than me.

The jolt of the landing shook my bones and I rolled onto my side, then jumped up and cut the chute loose, pushing away the thick grass stalks and blades. I balled up the chute, like in training. It got hung on the tall grass, but I cut it free. I stashed the chute in a hole that was full of water and grass roots.

I had shit inside my flight suit. The shit was smashed inside the tight torso harness. I could not see past the tall grass all around me. In the spot where I had landed and rolled the grass was pushed aside and some was broken. I looked into the part of the dark sky I could see for some lights. The heat was intolerable, and bits of dust and flecks of duff from the rotten grass stuck to my wet face. At the base of the tall grass were roots that spread like corn roots back home, and the dirt was black and sticky. I unbuttoned my survival vest and loosened the straps on the torso harness and reached into my loose flight suit and peeled the smashed turds off the skin of my ass and threw them into the hole where my chute was floating. I took the bandanna from around my neck. I had worn it on two hundred and eighteen missions. I wiped my ass and threw the bandanna into the hole with the shit and the chute. I picked up the bandanna—it had been with me so long—but I threw it back into the hole. It stunk.

I crawled toward the high ground. They taught us to keep a low profile. The only noise was me crawling. I came to a small clearing on some flat rocks. Above the darkness of the grass I saw a mountain, a shadow of broken karst ridges and a tall jungle canopy against the black sky. I came to some rocks at the edge of the grass where the jungle canopy began. The rocks were high enough so I could climb them to above the tops of the grass. They had taught us not to hurry. The karst rock was brittle and pointed and black. The grass and the jungle canopy met at the base of the karst ridge. I could crawl along the tops of the rocks, in and out of the grass and the jungle canopy, and climb out of the valley toward a saddle in the mountains that would lead to the south. I tried to be quiet but thought I was loud. There was no noise except for me. Across the valley, to the south, was another mountain of karst ridges.

They taught us not to crawl fast. As I crawled I found a cave in the rocks, a cave I could see out of that would not be seen from the valley. I was able to move quietly. I crawled into the cave, ass first, and I drank from my can of water. I was breathing hard. I had a revolver. I had food, water, a knife, first-aid and sewing pouches, a good flight suit, the blood chit, a radio. No watch. Pete always wore a watch. He told me I was stupid for not wearing a watch.

The cave was more of a schism in the rocks than a cave, was not like a room. I had gone in ass first between some rocks, into the opening of the schism. I was right side up, but jagged rocks were under my ass when I set my weight, so I shifted to one side, got the jagged rocks off my ass, and rested on a flat rock surface on my side. I could see out but there was no moon. It was quiet except for my breathing. I did not like being on my side, so I backed in farther, across the jagged rocks, feeling my radio.

It is full dark. I am quiet. I stay still, cramped between rocks. I figure Pete is in the valley on the other side of the mountain behind me. We are sixty miles north of the DMZ, ten miles east of the Laotian border. My cave faces south. Pete will crawl north in the other valley and find a cave facing south like mine. Both of us facing south will set up the best rescue. Looking out of my cave I will see the rescue helicopters before Pete will. When they come I will get on the helicopter and we will go over and get Pete before we head back south to Da Nang. If they don't see me in the first rescue pass, they will see Pete in the next valley and they will all pick me up on the way south.

There was a hand-sized radio in my survival vest. I rotated the volume knob to off and flipped the silent on switch, then eased the volume on. The voice was faint but clear. The squelch was out of adjustment, so there was some faint static. "This is Moonbeam on guard to all aircraft: avoid x-ray charlie six-six-zero-niner-four-zero on the two-two-eight-degree radial at four-eight nautical miles; channel one-zero-three; until one-four-five-five zulu; avoid by ten nautical miles. Repeat: avoid x-ray charlie six-six-zero-niner-four-zero on the two-two-eight-degree radial at four-eight nautical miles; channel one-zero-three; until one-four-five-five zulu; avoid by ten nautical miles."

I keyed the mike. "Moonbeam: manual six-niner."

"Manual six-niner: read you weak and clear. Manual six-niner: if you read us, acknowledge with two clicks."

I clicked the mike twice.

"Moonbeam copy. If you have words on your wingman give me two clicks."

I clicked the mike twice.

"Moonbeam copy. Manual six-niner: were you working with Copperhead at the time you were hit?"

I clicked the mike twice.

"This is Moonbeam. Understand you were working with

Copperhead at the time you were hit." Two clicks. "Roger, six-niner. Save your batteries and remain concealed. Are you safe? ... Roger. Be advised maintain contact at zero-zero and three-zero past each hour. We have two aircraft in the area monitoring your position and your communication. Do you understand? ... Did you have any contact with your wingman at the time that you went down? ... "

I broadcast voice. "I believe he's in the valley north of me."

"Copy that. Save your batteries. We are now trying to monitor your wingman. We will be here all night. As best as you can estimate come up about every thirty minutes and we'll try to contact you. Present time is five-five past the hour, five minutes to one Hotel time. SAR will begin at zero-five-thirty, so you've got about four and one half hours to wait. SAR is organized except for clearance. If you haven't already, get your water down and stay hid as well as you can. I'm sure you understand the position you're in, a real hot area. It's likely to be a long SAR for you. There will be a comm relay in the area all night. Dig in. We will monitor guard and we'll talk to you next time you're up. Moonbeam out."

The UHF radio was the size of a fat paperback, dull dark green with two knobs and a retractable antenna. The radio was on one end of a piece of nylon twine; the other end of the twine was tied inside my survival vest so the radio could not be lost. After I moved backward farther into the cave I was able to sit more upright, though I was cramped by a rock overhead. The darkness made the heat seem out of place. I had sweated so much my skin had an oily film, slick and stinky, that made my flight suit feel like oilcloth. The rocks were hot and made me even slicker. I slid over and between the rocks on my ass and my back. I held the radio in one hand, the survival vest in the other as I slid around and found my place. There was no difference between the darkness of the cave and the darkness outside.

I feel a presence in the cave, another being. I look and glance aside from where I am looking. Uncle Goody taught me how to glance aside instead of looking straight at something in the dark.

He told me about these little things inside your eyes so if you look straight at something at night it can't be seen, but if you glance aside the little things work better and you can see. When I glance aside it is too dark to see anything, but there is something there. I sit still with my knees up in front of my face with my arms around my knees, my wrists clasped, my head bent forward bowed, so it is hard to swallow. I am breathing hard but trying to be quiet. I am leaning back against a rock. Uncle Goody told me glancing aside was good if you were trying to walk through the woods at night, or if you were plowing a mule at night because the daytime was just too hot to plow. I feel motion in the cave. The hair on my neck and arms is up. I shiver. I feel breath on my hand that holds the radio; then I feel a nibbling on my fingers. I sit still and hold my breath. My chest is full of air. It is small, fast nibbling. A rat. He's big. I feel him. He is as big as a cat.

I figured five minutes had passed and I should contact Moonbeam on guard on the hour. I moved my hand with the radio on it and the rat backed away. I felt his presence but not the nibbling or the breath. I turned the volume all the way down and flipped the on switch. I eased the volume up slowly. There was no static. I eased the volume up high and put my other hand on the squelch in case the static started. There was no static. I mashed the transmit button. "Moonbeam: manual six-niner." There was no static when I mashed the button. "Moonbeam: manual six-niner." There was a press-to-test button, a way to check the batteries. I pressed the button. There was no light. There was no power. "Moonbeam: manual six-niner." I rested my hand with the radio on the rock. I leaned back against the rock and used my thumb to turn the volume knob down and turn the radio off. I felt the breathing and held my hand still; then I felt the nibbling on my fingers. Pete and I had eaten a can of sardines before we left our hootch, while we were drinking Jack Daniel's, before we went to the bar for our usual martinis, before we went to fly. I hadn't washed my hands.

Maybe I should put my gloves on. They are in the zippered

pouch on my flight suit. The rat will go away. The radio is dead. My shoulders and elbows are drawn together in front of me and my knees bend toward my chin. I crouch in a tight ball in the schism. I open my mouth and exhale but there is no breath. I relax and pull myself into a tighter ball and suck in air and try again, but there is no noise. The scream comes again and again. I am conscious of my condition and I am embarrassed, thinking someone might see me trying to scream in a tight ball and worrying that they might not like me because of what I am doing. I scream until my throat will not make any more noise. Then I lay on the rock until my consciousness returns and I am aware someone might be watching, and I control myself and relax.

They never taught me how to flip a rat, but I learned. You let him nibble on your fingertips and you lay still. You let him crawl up your body to your lips and nibble some there and you lay still. Then you flip him as hard as you can, as far as you can, and you sleep for a few minutes before he wakes you up nibbling on your fingertips. He stays gone longer if you wait for him to nibble your lips before you flip him.

The first sign of day was the rat singing. He stopped nibbling and sang in a drawn-out squeak. He ran around the cave, running across me but not stopping. I slept some as soon as I was used to him running on me, as soon as I knew he was not going to stop and nibble. When I woke I changed my position. My legs and skin were asleep from being cramped against the rock in the cave. Black turned to deep grey. More heat settled in the cave as soon as the dark was broken. I drank another sack of water and hunkered for the wait. The rat quit singing and was still. Birds took control of the jungle early, loud at first, establishing order, then settling about their business. A small river worked through the other side of the valley, across the grassy plain where I had landed, and beyond the small river karst ridges rose fast from the valley. The view was framed by the rocks around the opening of my cave. The rocks were shaded inside, and the light outside, even before the sun broke from the horizon, was brilliant. As the cave got hotter I sweated and stunk and the rat went away.

All my gear is good except the radio. I am facing south. The sun is to my left. It is so bright it hurts my eyes to look out. They taught us moss grows only on the north sides of trees and rocks. I will be able to verify my direction at night feeling trees. There are plenty of vines and plants. I will find caves or schisms in the rocks and sleep in the heat of day facing south. They taught us to sit tight the first day on the south slope of a ridge if the radio went dead. They said if the rescue came it would come to the last place they had a fix. They said if we sat still and they could get clearance for the rescue they would come. Pete is in the valley to the north. He is there if he went in. Maybe he did not go in. Maybe he went back to Da Nang.

I kept a count of the days in my head for ten days, then I found a nice hard stick that would fit into the pocket on my flight suit and used my knife to notch the stick every time the sun came up. I moved at night to the south; I slept during the day. I knew I had bombed some of the ridges I crossed when I moved south at night. They looked different from the ground.

I was not sure where I was until night one hundred and eight. That was when I heard a noise. The noise had to be coming from a waterfall, water gushing over rocks, then free-falling, then splattering on rocks. The deep background roar told me it was a big waterfall. I was moving to the south, and the noise was faint at first. It was night. I moved some more, then stopped, and the noise was louder. It was a big waterfall. It was a full night's movement away. I figured the waterfall was the one I had seen flying with Pete on an armed reconnaissance hop. That would put me close to Laos, just one ridge north of the DMZ. The waterfall was too far away to get to in one night. I knew where it was. I had seen it before. I found a ledge on a cliff I was working and settled in the shade where I could spend the day. The noise of the waterfall was a real good thing. I drank a can of water and sniffed some brown powder and settled in for the day.

Pete and I had seen the waterfall from the air on an interdiction and armed reconnaissance mission. The reconnaissance birds would come in with pictures of what the intelligence people said were truck parks and ammo dumps in the jungle. We went out during the day and hit where Gunny Joe and his intelligence people said to hit. We carried thousand-pounders with daisy-cutter fuses that made the bombs go off above the ground, bombs suited for people and vehicles. We rolled in low on our interdiction target, ten-degree dives in combat spread, one pass. We dropped, and both of us did our victory rolls and hauled ass low to beat the big shock waves from the thousand-pounders. The gooks were asleep during the day, and they were scared to put their guns outside their big caves deep in the valleys. We never hit much on the interdiction hops, but we never got shot down. After we dropped we stayed low and we went sightseeing, flying low and fast through the canyons and valleys. That's when we saw the waterfall.

I am on my side on the ledge. The jungle canopy reaches above me. I am hidden from the jungle floor. At each dawn I try to see the first grey. If I sniff some brown powder I can usually detect the first grey. But when I sniff the brown powder I can't sleep in the early hours of the day, and the afternoons are too hot. The thunderstorms come in the afternoons but cool the air only until they pass. One night I saw flashes from bombing, I am that close to the border. I marked it on my stick. I feel the notches. There are a hundred and eight notches on the stick. Notch seventy-nine was when I saw the light from bombing. I was at the top of a karst ridge starting down a south slope when I saw the light to the west. Somebody was dive-bombing. It was not the giant walking through the dark jungle stepping on firecrackers. That happened two karst ridges back.

I have never moved in the daylight, though the gooks are asleep.

But I want to see the waterfall because it sounds so strong and the noise never changes. No matter what other noise there is—birds in the morning, thunder in the afternoon—the noise from the waterfall is constant. I open my bag of brown powder and sniff a pinch. I have to save some brown powder in case I meet up with Pete. He might need some.

Pete and I were sightseeing when we saw the waterfall. Pete was flying combat spread, high and to the rear. He was looking past me at the ground and ahead and behind for MiGs. I was navigating and looking for targets. We were out shopping around. That part of the hop was called armed reconnaissance. We could destroy anything we wanted to. Our birds were armed. We were both hot, ready to shoot anything. We switched our UHF to Winchester. I turned into a canyon near the base of a karst ridge. We were low and fast. It was a hot, bright day. I looked ahead into the canyon and there was the beautiful waterfall. I called "Vertical!" as I pulled straight up because Pete wasn't watching where we were going; he was watching me and looking for guns. He pulled up, blind. He lost me under his belly. Then he did a one-eighty roll and there I was, right straight above his canopy. I had been watching his belly in the pull up, thinking to him, telling him in my mind to roll one-eighty so he could see me and know where I was and that we were still together. I looked straight up, into Pete's cockpit, and he was looking straight up at me. We were both going straight up, bleeding airspeed, gaining altitude. He waved. I did a negative pushover and he Immelmanned and we leveled over the river on top of the plateau. We were canopy to canopy. We had lost most of our airspeed. Pete was inverted and did a slow roll and dropped down beside me so we were side by side, skimming the flat plateau. I asked him if he saw the waterfall and he nodded his head. "Safe!" I called, and we pulled our master arm switches to off.

I can see the grey. I should have thanked that gook for the brown powder. The brown powder is what makes me see the grey. So I know when the dawn begins. The gook pissed me off. Why couldn't he let me have some food? He had to be greedy and not let me have his food. He could have gotten some more food but I didn't know anybody in the area. If I had been in Hepzebiah Community I could have gotten food anywhere. I know all those people. If he had been in Hepzebiah Community I would have helped him get food. But around here I don't know anybody. But the gook knows these folks. He should have given me what food he had and gotten himself some more.

Day twenty-four. I check my stick. That first gook was day twenty-four. I had been eating plants and getting water from vines like they taught me, but I was so hungry. The gook just happened along. He came down the trail by himself. He reminded me of a fox I had seen when I went hunting on the ol' Hainted Place with Josh, one of Uncle Goody's boys. The fox came along a wildlife trail in a beech bottom. Josh and I were on a hill, between two gum trees, waiting for a squirrel. We were thirteen. The fox was trotting. I couldn't help but think he was whistling or humming to himself, he had such a spring in his step. We lay still and watched as he trotted by below. When I saw the gook trotting along the trail, I waited until he came close to me and jumped him from behind. He was wearing a huge pack that made him top-heavy. I dragged him into the bush and sat on his pack and pressed him into the ground face first. I held him still and told him I just wanted food. He tried to fight me. I grabbed his food pouch. He fought me, so I cut his throat. I cut it across the front, across his windpipe. He grabbed his throat, then he died. I went through his things. His pack was full of fifty-caliber ammunition. I took his food and some brown powder and I cut off his ear because he wouldn't give me any food. I got his food, and I got his brown powder. I wish I'd kept him alive so I'd have somebody to talk to. But he wouldn't quit fighting. He probably would have come around, been nice about it and not tried to get away. I could give him a little snort of the brown powder and me and him could sit around and watch the dawn, see who could see the first grey. Whoever sees the first grey gets an extra dose of brown powder. I should have thanked that gook. I've still got his ear. The first few days I had the ear I let it dry in the sun while I slept, then I put it in the sack with the brown powder at night while I was working my way south. He just happened along. The powder makes the jungle belong to me.

Pete and I were flying over the plateau after we'd seen the waterfall. We disarmed our airplanes and picked up some airspeed. As I was about to turn I saw a plantation on the flat horizon. There were acres and acres of rows of trees—I couldn't tell from the air what kind of trees. The river snaked through the acres of trees on its way to the waterfall behind us. The trees around the edges of the plantation were grown over by the jungle, but in the center of the plantation the undergrowth was not yet established. There was a plantation house, a French villa, with arched garden walls around courtyards and a massive living area with a terra-cotta roof. The garden walls and roof were pocked by bombs and fires, but the walls of the living area and most of the roof were intact. Pete and I went into our turn directly over the plantation. We were two hundred feet above it carrying five hundred knots. I pointed down in the turn and Pete nodded. We did a one-eighty and followed the river downstream to the waterfall. There was a thousand-foot drop at the fall. As we crossed the drop I gave Pete the arming signal and we armed our airplanes and rode south, toward the border and the DMZ. On the way we paused long enough to shoot our rockets at suspected truck parks, suspected bends in the river.

I want to see the waterfall because it sounds so strong and the sound never changes. I open my bag of brown powder and sniff a little pinch. I have to save some in case I meet up with Pete. I have never moved in the daylight, though the gooks are asleep. I want to see the waterfall. I will move during the day. I move by sight, using my pilot's eye to scan the terrain after every move. You learn to scan, move your head in regular patterns, looking at everything but concentrating on nothing. Then you keep scanning but start analyzing what you're looking at. Something will show up different from the previous scan—that's movement, that's where you look. The brown powder helps. I'd love to fly with the brown powder when I get back. They probably won't let me. They've probably got a rule against it, like we weren't supposed to drink before we left Da Nang. I can see anything that moves. I can see wind currents moving through the canopy; they increase their speed as the day gets hotter and the tropical trees begin to sway. The currents go up through the canopy; then the thunderstorms roll in hot and blast down on the canopy. As I move during the day the storm is less important than when I used to try to sleep during the day. It is tedious, moving and scanning. The thunderstorm tells me it is afternoon. I move into the canyon, staying away from the riverbank, moving and scanning. I am shielded from the valley by the canopy below, moving at the base of the rocks. The thunderstorm has passed and the noise of the waterfall is immense. I am traveling west, into the canyon where the waterfall stays. My flight suit has rotted knees and armpits and my untrimmed hair is matted on my shoulders and face. The gook trails are below the canopy. I got to get me a gook before I go to the waterfall. I need some food, and my brown powder is almost gone. I rub karst mud on my face and where my skin shows through the rotted flight suit. *Knife. Blood chit. Brown sack with ear. Stick. Boots and suit.* I go through the canopy into the jungle, moving and scanning. I go toward the river. The gooks bathe in the river at dusk.

I move beneath the canopy on the jungle floor, down the steep grade toward the river, and I come to the trail. The trail is parallel to the river and I come upon it in a straightaway. The trail is wide enough for one truck. It is paved with stones in mud. It is late afternoon. I scan both ways, then jump across the trail, bounding like a deer. On the low side of the trail I slide down and scan as I reenter the jungle, sliding downhill in the duff.

The soldier is squatting and shitting. I see that my momentum will put me on the soldier. My knife is ready and I meet the soldier as he uncoils from the shitting squat. My knife goes into his chest. I cover him with my body and scan uphill toward the trail. He is gasping. I look at the soldier's pack. Twenty-three-millimeter antiaircraft, Chinese. The soldier is bleeding on my flight suit. I roll away. The soldier is a girl. I feel her little breasts. She is warm. Her black pajamas are loose around her ankles. Her chest is bleeding and I am hovering over her. We are just below the trail. I move my bloodied hand to her stomach. She is moving. Her legs spread and I rub her crotch.

The soldier kicks. I put my bloodied hand over her mouth and squeeze her throat with my left hand. She knees me with both knees and frees a foot from the pajamas around her ankles and uses that free foot to kick at me. Her bleeding increases. She coughs. We are close to the trail on the low side, toward the river. I drag her down the hill, away from the trail. She is naked except for her top and I am dragging her by her head with both my hands. The undergrowth on the jungle floor is sparse under the canopy, but the duff is thick and soft. I break through the duff at times, stumbling in my crawl, as I pull the soldier toward the river. She bites my hand and I release her mouth and come back to hit her with my fist. Her teeth are gapped and rotting; she smells like betel nut; her eyes are red and glisten like mine.

She tries to grab my knife. I stab her again. She looks into me. I pull the knife out and drop the knife and put my bloodied hand into her crotch. She is wet and soft. I smell her; she is not moving. I rip the pajama top away. She moves slightly and her legs spread. Her eyes are closed. I pull the zipper on my flight suit and go into her. She relaxes. She was small, her legs spread and she relaxed.

I clear the peak of a karst ridge in the middle of the night. It has taken a week to climb, moving at night. For the rest of the darkness I move downhill, working the bare face of karst rock and through some hill vegetation. When the black turns to grey I settle on a face where I will be in the shade all day and sniff some brown powder. As the sun lights the valley I use my knife to put notch one-fifteen in the stick. The notches are small and the stick is brown and oily from rubbing my body. I put the stick back in the pocket. I keep it in the only pocket of my flight suit with no holes and a good zipper, the pocket with the ear and the pouch of brown powder.

I heard the *wop-wop* of the blades. I ran to an open ridge that was flat and ran parallel to the face of the mountain. The ridge stuck out and could be seen from the valley. I had thought every day of the procedures to follow. I unfolded the blood chit from around my waist inside my flight suit. The blood chit was stained and soiled, but the red print, in six languages, and the American flag stood out against the background of the stains. I saw the helicopter. It was traveling up the valley following the river. When I saw the chopper I waved the blood chit. I screamed. As the *wop-wop* got louder I rushed to the edge of the ridge, waving the blood chit. I threw the bag of brown powder off the cliff. The helicopter continued up the river. The engine did not change its tone. It kept going straight. I felt the wind and smelled the air. The pilot set up for a downwind approach, turning toward me, gaining altitude. I waved the blood chit. The mountain was deep green below me and alive with birds. The plain by the river was the triple canopy where I had been. The helicopter could drop me a line. I had practiced so many times. The helicopter came toward me from above. I saw the machine gunner in the open door. It looked like a fifty-cal pointed at me. The helicopter came closer and I felt the wind from the rotors. A line dropped from a winch outside the door. I tied the blood chit around my waist and waited for the crewman to guide the collar at the end of the line into the rock, and I ran to where the collar touched the rock and put the collar around me and held on while the helicopter lifted off and the winch pulled me up to the winch arm. A crewman helped me into the helicopter.

The other crewman on the helicopter looked over the machine gun that was trained on the canopy in the valley as we lifted off. I lay on the metal floor, curled in a ball. The crewman who had helped me manned his machine gun at the door I had come through. When we got to altitude the crewmen relaxed over their machine guns and loosened their helmets and moved the mikes away from their lips. I sat up and shoved the blood chit toward a crewman.

"We do this for a living, sir." The noise of the engine and the air made him shout. "Keep it—give it to your grandchildren."

The other crewman said, "Sell it on the black market. You can get five grand. How long you been out there?"

"A hundred and fifteen nights!" I showed him my stick. The *wop-wop* was in sync with the vibration of the helicopter.

Both crewmen stared at me. One of the pilots leaned back and spoke. "Where'd you go down?"

"North of Mu Gia."

"You're the one who got the guns."

"Did they find my wingman?"

One of the crewmen said, "Your wingman didn't go in, sir."

The pilot who was leaning back said, "Naw. This is the one where both of them went in and they put us on alert. Nobody ever found either one of them."

I asked him, "You been looking all this time?"

"Never did look. Never got clearance to look. Both of you went in, didn't you?"

"I don't know if my wingman went in or not. They never launched the rescue?"

The crewman said, "That's right." He looked at the other crewman and said, "That was a different one, when one of the birds went in and the other one didn't." He looked at me. "You got those fucking guns, though."

"How did you know to come get me today?"

"We were just sightseeing, just cruising around. Saw you wave. It's our regular patrol over the Z."

The pilot called ahead to Da Nang. I gave him my name and serial number.

The crewman asked, "Don't you want a clean flight suit, sir?"

"I'll wear this one," I said.

* * *

A jeep driven by a young private who had just arrived in-country took me to the operations bunker. The driver never looked at me. He looked scared until he left me on the asphalt road by the operations bunker. I walked across the wooden catwalk. It was afternoon; the thunderstorms were rolling in. The entrance to the bunker was like a cave, down the steps into the tunnel and the briefing room. The maps still hung on the walls with the borders of countries in red and the targets for that night in black. Some men in flight suits were smoking. They all looked at me. Someone coughed. An Air Force general in his khaki uniform was standing beside Gunny Joe. I had never seen an Air Force general before.

"Lieutenant Hardy?"

I stopped in front of the general. "Sir?" I smelled awful.

"Why did you fly over North Vietnam?"

"Sir?"

"You heard me, Lieutenant." Another person in the room coughed, and some people shuffled about. Gunny Joe was staring at me. "What'd you do, get lost up there?" the general asked.

I smelled awful and had rotten places in my flight suit.

Gunny Joe was stone-faced, the same way he had been the night I arrived at Da Nang, the night of the Kent State party. "Don't you want a new flight suit, Lieutenant Hardy?" he asked. "I can go over to the flight equipment room and get you a new flight suit."

"You wait, Sergeant," the general said. "How about it, Lieutenant?"

I said, "We briefed to go to the closest water if anybody got hit, sir."

"The North Vietnamese called the UPI and said we had violated our agreement. The people in Geneva had to explain to the world."

"We got the guns, sir."

John Rossi walked in, hurrying. He had been promoted to colonel. He told the Air Force general that he would get a debrief but I needed to get a good medical check. I gave Colonel Rossi the blood chit, but he gave it back to me and told me to hang on to it.

* * *

They took me to the hospital on the hill overlooking Da Nang. I was in a bed beside a marine from South Korea who had a hundred and twenty-two holes in him from grenades. They did not think he would make it, but they said I was healthier than they would have thought after such a long time missing in the jungle. I told them I was never missing, I was there all the time. They said what mattered was why I was so healthy. I told them about survival school and the little Negritos who showed us how to get water out of vines and fix plants to eat so we could survive if we got shot down. They told me I was too healthy to have lived off plants and water, so I told them about taking food from soldiers who came down the trail alone. Colonel Rossi talked to the doctors for a while. The marine from South Korea in the bed next to me went into a seizure and died.

Colonel Rossi drove us down the hill to the base. It was getting dark. He wanted to go to the club so we could drink and celebrate, but I told him I wanted to take a break, maybe sit on a bunker for a while, so we went to Colonel Rossi's hootch and Colonel Rossi gave me a bottle of Jack Daniel's.

The bunker was between Colonel Rossi's Quonset hut and the group executive officer's Quonset hut. It was the nicest bunker in the officers' billeting area. The Quonset huts were thirty feet apart and the bunker took up all the space between them. It was like the operations bunker but smaller, cut into the earth, surrounded by fifty-five-gallon barrels full of sand, a flat roof of sand, and steps going down into the bunker. There was room on top for two lounge chairs. Colonel Rossi sat in one of the chairs and I sat in the other. I opened the bottle of Jack Daniel's and drank, swallowing hard.

"How did you get the clap, Truck?"

"Same way everybody else does."

"While you were missing?"

"I wasn't missing, sir. I was there all the time."

Colonel Rossi shifted his gaze from me, then back to me. "I can
cut you a set of orders to go home."

"I came here to fly, sir."

"How did you get the clap?"

"When did you get promoted, sir?"

"I took over the group last month. How did you get the clap?"

"I had to jump gooks to get their food. One of them was a woman.
Where's Pete?"

"He went in the same night you did."

"Are you still looking for him?"

"His wreckage never showed up on any pictures. We couldn't
get clearance to look up north. It's been over two months."

"*I* made it."

"How much did you drink before you went flying that day?"

"We had our usual martinis." I drank from the bottle.

"You're going to have to answer some hard questions, Truck. It
was tight around here when you violated that airspace."

Colonel Rossi asked me if I had a girlfriend. I thought of Momma
and Daddy and Beth and Uncle Goody and Son. Janie Blue was the
only girl I thought of. I told him, "No." He climbed off the bunker
and went to his jeep and brought another bottle of Jack Daniel's.
He opened the new bottle and drank.

"Did you kill that gook soldier?"

"Which one?"

"You killed more than one?"

I took a dried ear out of my pocket. He looked at it.

"Yes, sir," I said.

"The woman?"

"When did you stop looking for me?"

"We never really stopped. We didn't know where to concentrate.
We never got clearance to go up north."

"That helicopter just happened to come by today."

"We never stopped looking, Truck. We couldn't look where
you were."

The mountains and the harbor were like connect-the-dot lights. Airplanes dropped flares which dangled from little parachutes and lit up the countryside. I turned up the empty whiskey bottle and licked the rim, then squinted with one eye and looked through the bottle with the other. Da Nang looked just like Paris.

"I need to know whether to put you back on flight status or cut you a set of orders back to the world."

"I could use some time away, sir. I want to go where there are big white people and whiskey."

AUSTRALIA
APRIL 1971

Most of the men were like me, hollow-eyed and tired, late teens and early twenties, in ill-fitting uniforms that had been packed for months. We cheered when we left the ground at Da Nang, then sat quietly for hours looking out the windows at the dark and watching the stewardess and imagining things about her. The cabin of the jetliner was stripped of its partitions, so we were all the same, in rows of seats, two hundred of us.

There was nothing but dark outside until we passed over Borneo sprinkled with dim glows from cook fires of the natives; then several hours later we saw a nest of light with irregular strings of white dots on either side, and we watched while the lights became separate and distinct and brighter until we could see the depth and life of the city, the highways, moving lights.

The stewardess stood at the end of the aisle at the front and told us we would be on the ground at Darwin for an hour, and we landed. The bar there was an open area covering most of the terminal, a concrete-and-metal building with small tables and cheap straight chairs cramped together and a counter on three walls; the other wall, of glass, looked out toward the lights, our airplane, and the runways. The healthy, smiling people who ran the place had beer in mugs on each table and several hundred more mugs of beer on the counters waiting for us. A dozen of these people were scattered around the room, smiling, collecting dollars. We sucked the beer and paid for it and stood in line to use the men's room and circulated around the crowded, noisy room, talking.

I stood at the counter next to an Air Force sergeant. "You going to King's Cross, sir?" he said.

"Haven't decided yet."

"You ever had a basket fuck, sir?"

"I'm not sure." I drank a beer, chugging without stopping to breathe.

"Well, you know what it is, don't you?"

"Seems like I heard some of the fellows who went to Bangkok talking about it."

"That's right, sir. I went to Bangkok on my first R and R. See, this is my second R and R. It was six bucks in Bangkok. You see, sir, you lay on your back on this single bed, and this girl comes and rubs your dick. They got this big woven basket that hangs from the ceiling by a chain. After she gets your dick big she climbs in the basket and spreads her legs, and there's a hole in the bottom of the basket, and this other girl winds up the basket, twists it on the chain so the basket rises up and won't twist anymore. Then you slip your dick through the hole in the basket into that girl in the basket—she's all squatted down and greased up. And they let go of the basket and it starts spinning around, and your dick is up in that girl spinning. I tell you what, sir—it'll take you away."

"Why didn't you go back there?"

"If you been there the next place to go is King's Cross. That's the word." He held his beer up, like he was toasting me, and turned and walked away.

I drank six beers at the bar by myself, sucking them all down fast, and I peed and got back on the plane with the rest of the men and flew toward Sydney. The men became animated after the airliner leveled at altitude, and they shucked their blouses. We started talking and moving around the cabin. There was a constant line at the pisser and we sang as we got closer and everybody smoked.

Most of the men knew someone who had been to Sydney, and everybody agreed, "You go downtown to King's Cross and rent a room and meet women who are pretty and nice who will sleep with you all week if you take them places and buy them food." They said the food was good.

At the airport they opened my bag and went through all my stuff. They opened my shaving kit and looked at my toothbrush, but they passed me quickly. They put us on buses as the black turned to grey, and we went to a processing center downtown. Sydney was big. It was a city. It could have been Trenton or Seattle or even Houston, except everything was clean. No litter. No rundown houses. At the processing center a colonel joked about getting the clap and explained about money and contraband and what to do if we got arrested. Then a big partition on one side of the room was moved and merchants had bought hundreds of suits and shirts and shoes and they wanted to rent the clothes to us cheap. I picked a blue suit that smelled clean and fit okay and five white shirts, the formal kind. Once the merchants were paid we were turned loose to take a free bus to King's Cross or hire a taxi for anywhere, as long as we were back in seven days.

I hailed a cab and got up front beside the driver. He was an older fellow, trim, tanned, with a short grey beard, and he looked me in the eye. He asked me if I wanted King's Cross, and I told him I'd like to find a nice room overlooking some water where there were no American servicemen. He clicked his meter and started talking, looking more at me than the roads. They drove on the wrong side of the road, and at every intersection I tried to figure who would do what next. He told me about being in the Aussie Merchant Marine during the war and how dangerous it was when the Japs got after them. He started naming some of his shipmates and telling me what happened to them after the war.

He took me to Bondi Beach, where rocky cliffs formed a horseshoe shape around a harbor. The beach was at the top of the

horseshoe, a wide beach of clear sand where breakers were
pounding the short cliffs that circled toward the sea from both ends
of the beach. There were some rock outcroppings on the beach.
On the little streets were shops and flats and houses like I had seen
in movies about Europe, with white picket fences, no signs, and
only a few people moving around on the November spring day. The
wind was picking spray from the breakers on the beach and
blowing it, sticky, on everything that sat still. The sky was overcast
with some low, fast-moving, ragged clouds.

I thanked the driver and gave him some money. I crossed the
street and took a room in a place called The Cliffs. It was stone. The
stone had been cut from the cliffs. The rooms were pretty inside
and my room was at the top of the horseshoe, so I could see all of
the beach in both directions. The panes in the windows were
small, but windows covered all the wall toward the ocean. The
water was not deep enough for the harbor to have ships, only some
small sailboats, and a few with white sails were in the whitecaps
offshore, almost past the strait of the harbor. Below my row of
windows was a street, and a car went by every few minutes. I
couldn't see the cars, because my window was high above the
street, but I could hear them go by. I drank a pint of whiskey I got
from the man who owned the motel, who had served with
American marines during the war. He gave me the whiskey and
told me he was proud to meet me. I finished the pint of whiskey
before I saw the girl on the rock on the beach by herself.

I crossed the narrow street and went down stone steps toward
the beach. My blue suit was not heavy enough for the cool wind
and spray, and I walked shivering with my hands in my pockets.
The ocean was loud. The sound was constant. The clouds were
heavy. There was no glare. The girl was sitting on a rock, a stone's
throw from the high water, reading a book, wrapped in a blanket
pulled over her head, with her feet tucked under her. She didn't
notice me until I was close by. I gave her a start. She tightened her
position under the blanket and her hold on the book.

"I thought you saw me coming."

"You're an American!" She spoke loud above the wind.

"Yes," I shouted. She was older, maybe mid-thirties, big grey eyes, ruddy complexion, and she had a nice smile, a wide face, a pretty face, a space between her front teeth, big lips.

"At Bondi Beach?"

"I told the cabbie I wanted to go somewhere away from all the servicemen."

We had to shout to hear. She looked at me and smiled. She closed the book, stood down from the rock, and loosened the part of the blanket around her head. A bronze-colored kerchief was tied behind her ears and across the top of her head. She shouted at me, "I'm Janet." She shook the blanket loose from her head. Her hair was thick and red like the kerchief.

"Are you an R-and-R person?"

"Fresh off the airplane," I said.

"There's talk around the hospital about R-and-R people who come by the planeload. Never at Bondi Beach."

"It's pretty. Guess it's nice in the summer, or winter, whichever you call the warm part of the year down here."

"Summer. The boaters come first, then the swimmers. I go to the mountains."

"I'm here for a week. Got any ideas where I should go?"

"There's a bar over there." She nodded toward the row of shops beyond the stone wall and the road. "Some blokes go there, friends I know."

"I'd thought about seeing some of the country."

"The trains are good. Aren't you freezing?"

"Yes."

"What do they call you?"

"Truck."

We walked together toward the stone wall; the green blanket with the flowing red mane on top moved like it was being blown across the beach. "Why 'Truck'?"

"Ever since I was old enough to drive I've had a truck."

"Who started the name?"

"An old girlfriend."

"What was her name?"

"Judy."

"She's not your wife?"

"No."

We went to the base of the stone wall, out of the wind, where we could talk without shouting. We stood in the sand.

"Actually, I have a car now. It's a fifty-five Chevy. Ever seen one?"

"In the movies."

"Great machine. Got it from a little old lady who only drove it to the bank and the grocery store. Rebuilt the engine. Souped it up a little bit."

"When did you arrive?"

"Just this morning."

We were standing at the base of the stone wall. I was comfortable out of the wind. She was looking at me, her head tilted slightly back. She was studying me.

"I would say that you probably work on machinery."

"You mean at the war."

"Yes, at the war."

"I operate a machine."

"An airplane?"

I was glad she figured it out. "Every chance I get," I said.

"You enjoy what you do."

"I enjoy flying."

"I mean the other—the fighting."

"We get good missions."

"Do you ever think of the other side?"

"Not really."

We both looked out to sea, past the strait of the harbor.

"What's your real name?"

"Horace."

"You look more like 'Truck' but I prefer 'Horace.'"

"Some people call me one thing, some people call me the other."

"I'm a medical assistant. I enjoy it. It's important to enjoy what you do."

"I enjoy flying."

"My shift is off this week. Week on, week off."

"This will be the first week I've had off in a year."

"I was hoping you were a mechanic. My radiators clang so. They've been on all winter. They get clogged. Cleaning them out is at the top of my list for the week. Do you keep lists?"

"Sure do."

"My father taught me about working on cars. I've changed an intake manifold by myself."

"We use a lot of lists when we fly."

"My flat is two rooms and a bath. It's only a block from here, above the street."

"I'm at the Cliffs."

She kept the blanket around her, hiked up at the bottom so she could walk, and turned toward the stone steps that went to the street. We walked toward the street and the buildings as we chatted.

"What's it like in Vietnam?"

"It's not like anything. It's something all by itself."

Once we were on the sidewalk by the street we were in the wind again. I followed behind her and to the side on the narrow walk.

I asked her, "Do you work on your own car?"

"I have no car. I ride the bus."

The shops were closed tight in the wind but open for business. The brisk walk kept me warm. The shopkeepers glanced at us as we went past on the sidewalk. We crossed the street to a wider walk and walked fast, side by side.

Janet's flat was brick, with a brick stoop and a tile roof. There were four flats alike side by side in each building, several buildings in a row. There were some metal chairs on the stoop. I opened the door, shivering to keep warm, and she went in first. Pencil sketches of seascapes were hanging on walls and leaning on tables and whatnot stands. She unwrapped her blanket, and underneath was a white nurse's uniform, tailored for a good fit, with some small badges on the lapel and the name DeJean on a name pin. She was freckled and tan. I took off my blue coat. The room was warm and humid. I rolled the sleeves on my white shirt to just below my elbows. Her radiators clanged, and we jumped at the noise; then we both laughed.

We sat on an ornate Victorian couch that needed new upholstery. She said she was going to fix some tea. She got up and went toward the kitchen part of the room.

"Why did you come here?" she asked.

"I needed some time away."

"It's a good place to get away. My grandfather got away from Orléans, France," she told me. "He came to Australia with a portable, steam-driven sawmill and my grandmother and nothing else. He died when I was little. He was proud of his ancestry and all the money he made." She was at the sink by the stove. She put on some water and got out tea bags. "I remember him very well. He died in a fire in a whorehouse. He had gone to town to close a deal on a state contract and got carried away. My poor grandmother still hasn't gotten over it. She still laments 'Father's atrocity' to me everytime I see her."

"Did you ever see him run the mill?"

"Oh, yes."

"What kind of mill did he have?"

"A Frick. You know mills."

"Aught or double-aught?"

"Double-aught."

"Did your granddaddy have an edger?"

"He had two edgers," she said. "Two edgers save a lot of lumber. They were harder to run than one, but my grandfather explained to me once how in his lifetime that extra edger had saved enough lumber for him to make a profit instead of just breaking even during the bad times. Running two edgers made him a rich man, and that's what killed him in the end—the money."

* * *

Janet's bedroom was up tight, winding stairs and had a double-pitched ceiling. The window overlooked the ocean. During the daytime the view was not as good as the view from my room at the Cliffs, so we went to my room on the two pretty days.

On the days when it rained we went to her place. All the walls and both ceilings were covered with wallpaper, one kind, one pattern. It was red blossoms with yellow centers on blue foliage; at night when you couldn't see out the window, the wallpaper was all you could see.

On the morning of the third rainy day Janet came from her bathroom in a full-length gown. It had a low neck and loose armholes and a high waist. She had a way of looking at me while she walked, smiling with her face and eyes, that made me want her, want to take care of her. She got between the sheets. I switched off the light, stripped down to my green Marine Corps–issue skivvies. The room was dark because of the new storm outside. We both lay still for a few minutes, looking through the window. The wind was intense, an April storm. A street light some distance down the way gave just enough illumination to see a tree, some kind of tree, blowing in the force of the wind. Rain or spray was hitting the window in sporadic sheets. I reached for Janet and nudged her toward me. She took my hand and kissed it.

"Have you ever been to a whore?"

"No."

"Do you want to?"

"I never thought about it."

"I mean now. Do me like a whore."

"Okay, I will."

Every time I entered Janet was like the first time. I always came fast. She was so warm and wet and tight. Every time I came she came too. And every time she came she cried.

I asked, "You want me to cook another one of Truck Hardy's famous omelets?"

"Why do you have to leave at this time of day?"

"We have to leave so we get back there at night. The gooks ain't gonna blow away a planeload of vacationing GIs at night, because our people could see the flashes from their guns, and everybody on our side would be called out of bed to go out there and kill those gooks, and if the gooks got killed for shooting down a planeload of vacationing GIs at night they would lose, not because they would be dead but because they would lose the positions from which to operate. Do you want me to fix an omelet?"

"No." She was on her back with the sheet up to her neck. "Why do you have to fly so much?"

"I don't *have* to fly. I *want* to fly. I don't want Pete to get more missions than me. See, we got this bet: a case of Jack Daniel's says I get more missions than him. He was down when I left Da Nang, but he's probably back by now. They've probably found him by now. I know that asshole is flying twice a day while I'm down here. I've got two hundred and nineteen—figure I'll have to get fifty more to beat him. He'll have some time away too, like I did, so I'll fly twice a day while he's gone, then when he gets back there won't be enough days for him to catch up with me before we rotate home."

I looked at my watch and leaned to her and kissed her on the mouth.

She backed away. "I bet you can't do it again." She threw the sheet off. The front of her body was tight. Her breasts did not sag sideways when she lifted herself and lay resting on an elbow.

I rubbed her hair.

"Who's Pete?"

"He's my friend."

"I hope he's okay."

"Why do you always cry when you come?"

"I don't know why I cry. When will you have to fly again?"

"I'll never *have* to fly again. I hope to get to fly twice a day for a week to make up for the missions I've lost since I've been down here. I can't let Pete get ahead of me."

"You didn't tell me about Pete."

"No."

"People will shoot at you."

"Yeah. Or I might decide to go on home. Depends on what Pete's up to. I might just go on home."

Her john had a tank mounted high on the wall and you had to pull a chain to get the squatter to flush. There was a cast-iron tub on legs and a shower nozzle on the end of a rubber hose to hold in your hands. I shit and washed and shaved. The blue suit still smelled good and I put on one of the clean white shirts. Then I kissed Janet and used her phone to call a cab.

BOOK THREE

THE SECOND WAR

HEPZEBIAH
MAY 1971

The shades of green in the forests were a sharp contrast to the plowed fields' browns, greys, and rusts. The corn was big enough for the leaves to overlap between plants. The oats and wheat had turned brown. The tobacco fields were full of small, healthy bright-green plants in manicured, contoured rows: four rows of tobacco and a sled row, four rows of tobacco and a sled row. The country roads with their twists and turns and an occasional slow-moving car were spread in an endless, interlocking network of dirt and paved strips. The sacred lines of ownership, described in abstract mathematical and legal terms in some book somewhere, were shown on the ground by the straight tree lines and squared-off fields. They contrasted with the natural topography and the meandering streams.

The small towns were nestled in tight among the trees in the bright of early morning. The only real activity was on the main highways, where the rush-hour traffic was transferring people from the home part of their lives to the work part. The Delta DC-8 made a slow circling descent to intercept the approach corridor. I tried to spot Piedmont, following familiar landmarks to the horizon, but was on the wrong side of the tourist-class section.

I was wearing my officer's khaki uniform. I watched the city pass underneath, the university complex, shopping malls, new industries.

The final approach brought us over a four-lane highway, over the road signs and billboards. AIRPORT LEFT LANE was green and white. There was some congestion at the intersection. A big red billboard proclaimed that the City Bank had free checking. Another one told everyone to fly Delta. Another said, GET RIGHT WITH GOD. When I was in the jungle I promised, "If I get through this I'll do something worthwhile with the rest of my life."

I gave the pilot a six out of a possible ten for the landing: high, overpowered start, deceleration in close with a dive for the deck, but a smooth touchdown.

I sat in the front seat of the taxi. The middle-aged driver fired up a Marlboro. He had a splotchy beard and a beer gut.

"Lemme see. That's just off the highway, close to that new shopping center. Goddamn traffic's terrible around there this time of day. Goddamn traffic's terrible all over town this time of day. I can remember when you wouldn't see twenty cars a day out there on Ol' Mill Road. Now it's grille-to-ass all day long." He started the meter and eased off the ramp into the traffic. "Marine Corps? I was in the Navy back in the fifties. Used to have a helluva time with those marines. They was some mean bastards." He could drive without looking at the road.

"Yeah."

"Don't know what the hell's wrong with military people now. They can't seem to get their mess together. That Vietnam thing is a mess. Our boys can't do nothing right. If they was as mean as they was when I was in, they would whip them little bastards over there and come on back home. Ain't that right?"

"Yes, sir."

There were cars everywhere, all going like a bat out of hell to get somewhere. All these people were going about their merry ways, busy as bees humming around their hive. The drivers in the cars going in the opposite direction were preoccupied, oblivious to the fact that they were screaming along the surface of the earth, surrounded by other people who were preoccupied and equally oblivious and screaming.

". . . so we all went back to the ship and . . ."

I wished the driver would shut up and watch where he was going. The people driving in their cars were insurance salesmen and typists, delivery men and lawyers and factory workers, surveyors and clerks.

". . . course it wasn't always that way. Sometimes we had to wear our uniforms . . ."

We went by a shopping center. Women with packages were getting into new cars. There were plenty of parking spaces around the edge of the parking lot, but people were sitting in their cars with their air conditioners on, burning gasoline, waiting for somebody to vacate a space so they could park close to the buildings so they would not have to walk all the way across the parking lot. There were red, white, and blue triangular-shaped plastic flags strung on a rope between the light posts in the parking lot. There were intersections where cars were waiting in line for the lights to change.

We left the main highway on a ramp that ended in a stop light. The driver stopped talking. The traffic was bad on Old Mill Road. We drove a short distance, then turned into an entrance to some apartments. The sign said THE PIERS. There was a big rope around the sign and some netting and big corks across the top, just above the fake seagull. The parking lot was lined with creosote-treated posts that were driven into the ground like pilings. The driver stopped the cab. I gave him a ten and told him to keep the change.

I found 2387. A man came out of 2389 and got into a new Porsche. He was wearing a three-piece suit and fancy shoes. I pressed the doorbell and heard somebody walking inside the room. The door opened. Beth had on her housecoat, curlers in her hair, and no makeup. She put her arms around my neck and burst into tears, holding on to me a long time, like she would never let go.

I dropped the bag on the concrete stoop and buried her head in my arms and hands. "Hey, baby sister. I like your hair like that."

There was a laugh among the tears, then she cried harder and tightened her hold on me. She backed away finally and looked up into my face. "I didn't know if I'd ever see you again." I pulled out my red bandanna and wiped her eyes.

I handed her the bandanna. She turned and walked toward the couch, blowing her nose, and she sat and looked at me. I sat in the easy chair. Beth had buckteeth when she was little. My favorite picture of her, the one I had with me, was taken when she had buckteeth, in the sixth grade. Now she looked the same as the picture except her teeth were fixed. She was pretty, with a dimpled smile.

"I stayed home from work hoping you'd come today. I stayed home Tuesday and last Friday," Beth said.

"I don't like airport scenes."

"It's just been so long. You look good."

"How's Momma and Daddy?"

"Daddy's fine. Stays busy all the time. Momma's aged. She's had a rough year. Every day she hated to read the paper, but she read it. Every time a strange-looking car came down the road she sat at the kitchen table hoping nobody would knock on the kitchen door. Then when they did come and said you were missing . . . she prayed for a long time every day. But she's never talked to anybody about it. Daddy says she has nightmares."

The room had the same furniture from her last apartment, nice cushioned stuff, kind of formal.

"You got time to drive me out to the house?"

Beth stood. "Let me change clothes and fix my hair. You want something to drink? I bought some beer a couple of weeks ago, just for you." She went to the kitchen and came back with the beer. "I'll be ready in a few minutes." She started up the stairs, then stopped. "Thank God you're home, Truck." She shouted as she went up the steps, "You can cut the radio on if you want to."

I went to the console unit and pressed the button, then went back to the easy chair and popped the top on the beer and took a drink. ". . . that's what I always thought you were supposed to do. Let's see if any of the neighbors have anything to say about it. Thank you for calling."

"Goodbye, Wally."

"Goodbye. This is 'Ask Your Neighbor.' If you have any opinions, recipes, or thoughts you'd like to share with our listening audience, you can call us at 796-WADD, and we'll try to get you on the air. Now this . . ."

They ran a sixty-second spot on free checking at the City Bank. I drank the beer, looking at the traffic through the window in the back of the room.

"This is 'Ask Your Neighbor.' We have a caller on the line. Go ahead, please."

"Wally?"

"Go ahead, please. You're on the air."

"Wally, this is Mrs. Gladys Hamilton down in Covington?"

"Hello! I'm glad to know we have some listeners down near the coast."

"Well, I listen to your show every morning while I piddle around the kitchen? And I declare! I enjoy it *so* much."

"Thank you, Mrs. Hamilton."

"I'm calling about the lady who called in a few minutes ago, about whether you ought to wash a cast-iron skillet or not. I just want to say that I still use the very same skillet my grandmother used over fifty years ago, and that skillet has never been washed! All the people down here around Covington say that I cook the best fried chicken they've ever tasted, and it's all because of that skillet. My chicken tastes just like my grandmother's chicken did. I don't think you should ever wash a cast-iron skillet. I just wipe mine out with a rag."

"Thank you for calling, Mrs. Hamilton. Okay! Evidently just cleaning your skillet with a rag is good for your skillet, or at least it seems to have improved the quality of chicken down around Covington. This is 'Ask Your Neighbor.' You're on the air."

"Wally? That lady who just called about her frying pan and her grandmother's chicken? Well, the reason her fried chicken tastes like her grandmother's fried chicken is because it *is* her grandmother's fried chicken. Anybody who would go that long without washing what they cook in has got to be eating germs."

"Don't you think that heating the pan every time you cook in it would sorta sterilize it?"

"No way, Wally. If you don't wash your frying pan, you've got a dirty frying pan."

"Thank you for calling. Maybe some of our listeners will—"

I pressed the button and wandered to the window and looked out at the traffic. The light at the intersection turned red. The cars piled up, three lanes wide. The drivers sat in the cars looking straight ahead. There were new cars and old cars. There were all kinds of pickups and delivery vans, all colors. The light turned green. The cars started slowly, in sequence. Some turned, some went straight. Some cars had more than one person in them. I drank the last of the beer, went to the kitchen, pulled a fresh beer out of the refrigerator, and popped the top. I went back to the living room, took the newspaper off the coffee table, and sat in the easy chair. The front page was a couple of natural disasters, a murder, some corruption in state government, and a piece about a bombing raid in Vietnam. I turned to the editorial page:

TIME FOR OUR LEADERS TO LISTEN

When college students are shot to death on their campus by national guardsmen, when half a million people mass in Washington to present their case to our government, when continued efforts by our military forces and continued loss of our young men's lives seem to accomplish nothing, it is time for someone to notice the Vietnam debacle. If our nation hopes . . .

I turned to the funnies. The Phantom's treasure had been stolen from the Skull Cave and he was getting ready to whip somebody's ass. Little Henry sat under a tree. An apple fell on his head, so he put Band-Aids on the rest of the apples in the tree to keep them from falling. Snoopy was playing left field for the baseball team and fell down.

I looked at the horoscope, for Gemini: "Stay close to loved ones. Be prepared for a significant event."

Beth came down the stairs wearing a sun dress. She was wholesome, nothing fancy, with brown hair tied up loosely and small earrings. "We might cook some steaks on the grill for supper."

I stood.

"I thought we might—" Beth stopped. She stopped walking and talking and planning and thinking. "What do *you* want to do, Truck?"

I looked at Beth, then at the floor, then out the window at the traffic, then back at Beth. "I don't know."

She came to me and held me. "You can't imagine what we've been through." She pushed herself away and looked at my distorted, wet face. "And we can't imagine what you've been through."

Willard Mitchell was the mailman. The parsonage at Hepzebiah Baptist Church was halfway through his route. His car, with a yellow-and-white U.S. Mail sticker on the back, was in the driveway, idling. We parked on the grass. The pines and shrubs looked bigger, the grass looked greener. I left my bag in the car and went to the back door with Beth at my side. I opened the screen and pushed the solid wooden door open. Willard was sitting at the kitchen table with his postal-service hat cocked back on his head, drinking coffee.

Momma was sitting closer to the door. "Oh, my goodness! Horace is home! Beth, go get Daddy, he's in his office." She was moving things around on the table to make room.

Beth left and Willard stood, taking the last gulp of coffee. He put the cup on its saucer. I went to Momma and hugged her as she got up.

"You always surprise us. It's always such a surprise." She put her hand on my cheek. She touched my shoulder, then went back to my cheek. I kept my arm around her and shook hands with Willard. He straightened his hat. "Good to see you again, Truck. I'd better get back to my route."

"Don't run off," I said.

"I'd better go on. Thank you for the coffee, Mrs. Hardy." He walked to the door.

"You're welcome. Stop by again. I'll have the water on."

Willard closed the door behind him. I asked Momma if she would put my name in the pot for dinner. She put both her arms around me, resting her head on my chest so her head fit under my chin. Her hair had been starting to speckle with grey; now it was almost solid white, pinned up in a bun. Her glasses rested on her chest, held there by a silver chain I had given her for a birthday. She had on a dress she could wear to town. She rocked back and forth slightly, barely noticeably, crying it's-all-over tears. "I'd forgotten how big you are, Horace." She looked up at me. "I hope you don't have to go back." I hugged her. She was plump and awkward to hug.

I heard Daddy coming toward the kitchen, whistling "Rock of Ages." Then he walked into the room.

"Well, blow me down! I knew you'd be here by the weekend!" He was wearing the old coat, old tie, and white starched shirt that served as his uniform. "When did you get in?"

"Couple of hours ago."

"You're back early."

"They decided to send me on home."

We looked at each other. I released Momma and embraced Daddy. It was the first time I remembered hugging the man. Daddy held me tight and patted me on the back. Beth was standing by the door, watching quietly.

Momma started toward the refrigerator.

"Fix us something to drink, Momma," Daddy said. "What'll you have, Horace?"

I sat at the table; Daddy sat across from me, and Beth went to help Momma.

"Got any fruit juice?"

Momma pulled a quart mason jar from the refrigerator. "Orange. Just squeezed it this morning. Made some custard, too. And I've got yeast bread rising."

Daddy said, "I'll take custard, in a bowl." He turned to me. "Need any help getting your stuff out of the car?"

"I can get it later."

Momma looked at me and brought the drinks. The kitchen smelled like bread. The outside door was open, allowing the sound of a mockingbird to filter into the sounds of the conversation. It was warm. They all watched me. When I raised the glass to drink my hand shook.

Momma picked up a paper napkin and twisted it. "Several people in the church have asked about you. And Judy came to homecoming. She would like to see you."

Daddy asked, "Did you get your orders?"

"Cherry Point. My old CO, Colonel Rossi? He's down there. Wants me to be in his group."

"Do you plan—?"

"I plan to keep flying."

Daddy was eating custard, licking the spoon clean with each mouthful.

I said, "Thought I might buy me a piece of land, find a place to stay out here, somewhere nearby."

Daddy said, "The family reunion's in September. We've talked about going to the mountains for a week this summer. Beth might go. We've thought maybe if you wanted to go, we'd . . . all go."

"I might have to fly." I stared at the juice, rubbing the little beads of condensed moisture on the outside of the glass until a drop of water formed and ran down to the tablecloth. Momma had three tablecloths: a faded green-and-white-checkered one; one with red ribbons and birds and dogwood blossoms that had a patch in one corner where somebody had stuck a knife through it twenty years ago, and a Christmas one with holly and candles on it. The faded checkered one was on the table. "I guess I'll just wait and see."

Daddy stood. "I haven't touched James Louis since you left." He licked the spoon one more time and put it in the empty bowl.

The women got up and Beth said, "Why don't we fix dinner? You're bound to be hungry after flying all night."

"The bread smells good."

Momma smiled. "I'll make you a little loaf of your own and put extra butter on it. It's already risen, ready to go in the oven. Beth, Daddy got some good, sharp apples from Miss Nellie at church yesterday. Why don't you make a pie?"

Beth folded her hands under her chin, like she was praying, cocked her head slightly sideways, and spoke in her hard Southern brogue, "I always get to make the pies."

Daddy went out the back door.

I took the last sip of juice and stood. "There were a lot of times I wanted to call and listen to you talk. I missed hearing you talk."

Momma said, "Do you have to go back?"

"No."

Beth went to the sink. I went back through the big door, outside to the lawn on the side of the parsonage near the church. Daddy was walking to the storage shed in the backyard where a sheet covered a car under a low, narrow shelter. I caught up with him, and we removed the sheet, folded it, and put it aside.

Daddy walked around the machine, looking at it closely. "Tires need some air, and we'll have to get a new battery. I used the one we took out in my Buick."

I opened the hood. The high-powered mill was covered with chrome. "I'd like to get James Louis cranked, on the road today."

"I renewed the license and your insurance when it came due."

"Thanks."

He threw me a set of keys. I drove the big Buick. We backed out in the driveway and rode to the stop sign in silence, then turned onto Snakey Road, toward town.

"We might have to put some gas in those carburetors to get him going. You might need points and plugs."

I drove.

"I hope you can spend some time with your mother." He paused, looking out at a bean field. "We were always anxious for your next letter. How's your friend you liked to fly with?"

I slowed for a curve. "You mean Pete?"

"Pete."

"He's still there."

Daddy looked out the window.

When we got to the auto-parts place a man was paying for a set of shock absorbers. Daddy found a car-care-products display and picked up a new kind of paste wax. He inspected the can, then put it back. The man at the counter finished writing the cash ticket, pulled it off the roller in the little box, and handed it to the man with the new shock absorbers. "Thank you," the man behind the counter said, "hurry back." He was a little fellow with a broad smile and combed hair who I remembered from school, but no name came to mind. "Hello, Mister Hardy," he said. "Hello, Truck. Can I hep y'all?"

I stepped up to the counter. "I need a twelve-volt battery, heavy duty."

"Just got a batch in yesterday. Already got fluid in 'em, ready t' go." He went to the back room, picked up the box, and brought it back to the counter. "Cash or charge?"

Daddy stepped up to the counter. "I'll get it."

The man at the counter filled out the ticket. "Hat'n seen ya around lately, Truck."

"Been outa town."

"You in the service, ain't ya?"

"Yeah."

"Guaranteed for eighteen months." He tore the ticket off and handed it to me. Daddy laid the exact change on the counter.

The parsonage was to the north of the church. On the south side of the church was the cemetery, two acres of stones and markers. Behind the cemetery, at the edge of the wood, was the sexton's dwelling, a four-room shotgun tenant shack with a porch all the way across the front, where Uncle Goody stayed. The outside of the shack was covered with heavy tar paper with a brick design on it, an off-shade of red bricks drawn between crossing strips of black-painted joints. The tin roof was painted green. The chimney at the north end was hand-cut stone. Brilliant red geraniums were blooming in pots across the front of the porch.

Uncle Goody was sitting in a rocker. His overalls were worn, patched, and clean. The sun reflected off his skin as he squinted to see.

"Hey, Uncle Goody."

The old man's face beamed. "As I live 'n' breathe!" He looked up toward the sky where the church steeple pointed—"Praise the Lawd!"—then back at me. "You sho is a sight fo' po' eyes, boy. When'd you get home?"

"This morning." I walked onto his porch.

The old man got up slowly. "I ain't never been so glad t' see nobody in my life." I took the man's extended hand and gripped it firmly. It was a callused hand, big, warm, and gentle. "You sho is a sight, boy."

"Son here?"

"Inside. Lemme get 'im." Uncle Goody went into the shack while I walked to the door and held the screen open and caught the familiar smells of wood smoke, homemade soap, and sweat.

Son was strapped in the homemade wheelchair, dressed in poorly fitting work clothes with a towel tied around his neck. His hands were twisted in his lap; his head rested on one shoulder, nodding slightly as thick liquid worked its way out of his mouth onto the towel.

Uncle Goody pushed the wheelchair onto the porch and locked the wheels, then walked around to the front so Son could see him. "Look here, Son." He was shouting, looking straight into Son's face. "It be Hor'ce Junior!" Uncle Goody shouted. "He done come back."

Son's head rolled back until his face pointed straight up; then his head rolled to the side until it rested on his shoulder. The eyes wandered, unable to focus for any length of time.

I moved closer until I was bent beside Uncle Goody.

"It be Hor'ce Junior!"

Son's body shook as he moved his hands around in aimless motions. "Ooummm . . . aannh."

"He be 'memberin' you now."

Uncle Goody moved aside, and I stepped in front of Son.

"We got us a birthday real soon, me"—I pointed to myself, then to him—"and you! I brought you a birthday present."

I put a box on Son's lap and opened the folded top. Son rolled his head to look at his father, then worked it back toward me.

Uncle Goody said, "Op'n it up! It be a gif'! It be yourn!"

Son let his head rest on a shoulder and moved both hands in jerky motions until the twisted fingers were inside the box. He fumbled for a moment until white wrapping paper moved aside.

"It's a model of my airplane. I had a man make it especially for you. I told him about you and he made it special, carved it himself out of a special kind of wood they have on his island, a Philippine island. It's for you. Happy birthday."

Uncle Goody held Son's wrist with one hand and took the model with the other. He held the wooden plane up and the three of us looked at it as he moved it slowly through the air.

"It be what Hor'ce Junior do." He kept moving the model and turned to me. "Sumtime when I'z hearin' dem jets go by in the sky, I takes Son's chair an' rolls it down off'n the porch and takes 'im out in the yard an' leans 'im way back so he be lookin' up, an' I says, 'Son, dat's whut Hor'ce Junior do.' An' Son, he soon know'd whut it wuz I mean." He moved the model into Son's hands and let it rest there. "He be gettin' real 'cited now. We best set awhile so's he don't get all wo' out."

Son made noises, moving the model in his lap, and we went to the chairs.

As we sat, Uncle Goody smiled at me like I was one of his own. "I 'member the day you 'n' Son was bawn. I'z still stayin' on the Hainted Place, 'fore I done got too ol' t' tend to it. I know'd there wuz sumpin' wrong wi' dat youngun, an' Miss Callie, she lyin' there dead, kilt graveyard dead by the birthin' o' Son. Yo' Daddy, he left yo' momma in dat ol' pars'nage an' he come down there t' dat ol' shack whilst you wuz bein' bawn 'cause he'd heard we'd lost Miss Callie. He tol' me things was bad an' dey wuz gonna get worser, but God wuz gonna take care o' me an' all dem younguns. Won't for him, I'd of goed back in the holler an' stuck cold steel in the midst o' my heart, what wi' Miss Callie dead an' all dem younguns t' raise. An' all dem white church folks brung us'ns food an' clothes an' stove wood an' dey plows the cawn an' the cotton an' ast if'n dey anthing what I'z needin', me a po' nigger what's did nothin' but work hard an' make whiskey all my bawn days. Ever since dat day you an' Son wuz bawn, I ain't sweat none."

"How's the other children?"

"Kyle an' Evan finish school whilst you wuz gone. Dey all drops by an' heps me wi' Son, an' dey brings me food frum the sto' an' stuff I needs round dis ol' place. Dey scattered all 'mongst here an' younder, but dey stays up wi' me, don't ferget me."

Son made quiet noises while he played with the model.

Uncle Goody rocked in the chair and rubbed his big hand over his bald head. "Dey's younguns here on Sundays near 'bout all day. Dey'll be a'wantin' t' see ya." Then he looked at me and smiled. "I know'd ya'd make it. I done said a prayin' fer ya every evenin' ya' wuz gone. I know'd the Lawd wuz wid ya, know'd it wuz bad fer ya over der. Dey wouldn' let no niggers fight in dem wars when I'z a young buck, so I'z stayed right here an' tended the crops. But I'z knowin' it wuz bad fer ya."

I stood.

"Set a minute, boy. It's yo' birfday too." Uncle Goody walked off the front of the porch, stepping easy, and disappeared around the side of the house.

I sat and watched Son playing with the model, rubbing it, then lifting it off his lap with both hands and making a low, growling noise. I looked at the big tombstones up near the dirt road where I had hidden in ambush, waiting for the school bus to come in a cloud of dust in the mornings. I always waited until the bus was close, then jumped out with a stick in my hand and forced the driver to take me to school; Beth never liked the game but played sometimes to humor me.

The dirt road was where I had walked the mile and a half to Mister Alcie Pace's house every Monday afternoon to get a half-gallon of fresh buttermilk. Every time I went, once a week for years, he told me how he liked to tithe and the preacher always got 10 percent of the milk from his old saggy-boned cow. I was playing on the way home one day and dropped and broke the jar and hid in the woods until Momma and Daddy found me after dark, scared to go home because I had failed and wasted the buttermilk. I had watched it drain into the ditch.

Majestic oak trees stood on the church grounds and in front of the cemetery. The men from the church had planted them and said a prayer so they would grow big and strong and survive all the storms. At the church I had followed Uncle Goody while he worked in the yard and answered all the questions I could think to ask. I looked at Son in the wheelchair Uncle Goody had made out of two bicycle wheels, a pipe, and some old lumber. So many times Beth and a bunch of the kids who lived in this old shack had pushed Son down to the creek and shown him frogs and ferns and salamanders, and the stars when we went at night.

The other side of the church was where the old parsonage had been before it burned, where me and Beth and Momma were in the yard when a bull had gone crazy, got loose, and come running through, chasing us into the house; he banged his horns into the side of the parsonage until a bunch of men came with ropes and pulled the bull off the porch. They shot the bull in the front yard.

Uncle Goody came from the smokehouse, around the side of the porch, with a big salt-cured ham. There was no cover on the ham, no wrapping. "She'd littered twice," he said. "I 'llowed her t' get fat. Know'd you'd be wantin' a nice ham onest you come home from the war. Dis here's yer birfday gif'."

I walked to meet him and took the ham, then went onto the porch.

"Thank you for my present, Son."

Son rolled his head, then went back to playing with the model airplane.

James Louis started on the first try after I put the battery in. I let him idle, then eased onto the road. I kicked in the extra carburetors and James Louis came to life, responding with a surge of power. I drove on the dirt road to the corner at Snakey Road. The Justices ran a filling station at the corner, but it was closed because it was Wednesday afternoon and all the businesses closed on Wednesday afternoon so everybody could go fishing or work in their gardens or do something besides open their businesses. I put air in the tires and checked the oil and water, then I drove hard down Snakey Road.

Mister Alcie Pace's old home place was two rooms up, two rooms down, open the door and go to town, or that's what Mister Alcie had told me since I was little, and he would laugh at me when I looked like I did not understand. The old home place was off the road, down a dirt path, in a grove of giant oaks. The windowpanes were intact and the house was closed up tight. The weatherboard was painted, still in good condition. There were no curtains, and boxes were stacked inside big rooms.

When Mister Alcie's momma and daddy died he built a new house from a plan the *Progressive Farmer* included in a special housing edition in the fifties. Mister Alcie had showed me the picture and the plan in the magazine one day at church; then I watched the house grow, just like the picture, with clapboards and gables and dormers and a big front porch, green shutters and awnings at each window, and groomed shrubbery all around. Mister Alcie's new house was in front of the old home place, close to Snakey Road, a mile and a half from Hepzebiah Baptist Church.

I slowed James Louis when we were close to Mister Alcie's Place. Beside his new house, facing the road, was a square concrete-block building with a low-pitch roof. No signs, no windows. The blocks were painted white, the roof was black. There was enough room between the shoulder of the road and the block building for several vehicles. There was a rusted van with flowers painted all over it pulled up close to the door. The mufflers on James Louis had rusted some while I was gone, and the hard run down Snakey Road had blown out the pipes, so I left the pavement in a roll and skidded and stopped beside the van and raced the engine. James Louis sounded off, in tune, then sucked back, and there was a backfire when I cut the ignition. I heard the jukebox and got out of James Louis. The only music allowed at Mister Alcie's Place was Elvis and authentic country classics.

I pushed in the heavy metal door. The floor was finished concrete. The bar was homemade, cheap linoleum on a wood frame. Mister Alcie was behind the bar fiddling with the grill. Two men were sitting on stools drinking beer. I sat at the end of the bar. Neon beer signs were lit over the grill where the exhaust fan was blowing. Mister Alcie was scraping grease with a metal spatula and turned around and shook his head.

"Those bastards must be bad shots."

"They are. You got any cold beer?"

We shook hands.

"I've got all the cold beer you can drink." He reached into the cooler. "When'd you get home?"

"This morning."

He popped the top on the beer, then wiped the can with his rag and handed me the beer and wiped the top of the cooler. "Missed you around here, Truck."

I took a slug of cold beer. "Any of the regulars been around?"

"Not yet."

The two men at the bar were dressed sloppy in old clothes and had long hair. The bar was small. They were right there, watching and listening. I sipped the beer.

"Anything happen while I was gone?"

"Charlie got killed."

"Momma wrote and told me," I said. "She didn't tell me how."

"He was drunk. Driving Snakey Road. You know how they used to do?"

"Me and Charlie ran Snakey Road once."

"He'd just found out he had a high number in that draft lottery. Found out he wasn't gonna be drafted."

Mister Alcie leaned on the bar across from me. He was skinny and short, almost bald, and what hair was left was thin and grey, and his face was drawn with red lines. He always looked bored.

"Got broke into back in November. Had to put bars on the windows and buy that steel door. That's about it. Been kinda quiet."

I gulped the rest of the beer. "Lemme have another beer." I motioned to the two men who were watching. "And a couple for these fellows."

"Ah . . ." the one closest to me said. He shook his beer. "I still got some." He had a diamond stud in his left ear and his hair was clean and brushed on his shoulders.

The other man stared at a clock on the wall. "We don't want your fuckin' beer."

Mister Alcie pulled a beer out of the cooler and wiped it with the rag. He watched the two men.

"How many children did you kill over there?" the same man asked.

Mister Alcie reached under the bar and pulled out a Smith & Wesson .38 and laid the gun on the bar. Mister Alcie laid two small, rolled-up paper bags on the bar beside the gun. The first man put two hundred-dollar bills beside the gun, picked up the bags, and walked to the door.

The second man turned and said, "You people are all alike. All you understand is brute force." They left.

Mister Alcie dumped the leftover beer from the men's cans into the stainless-steel sink beside the grill and threw the cans into a barrel in the corner and wiped the bar. "Goddamn college students from the city." He pocketed the money. "They're all draft dodgers and queers. They like to mingle with the working class. The world's going to hell." He turned off the grill, the exhaust fan, all the lights except the neon beer sign behind the bar, and the jukebox. He bolted the door and took a case of cold beer out of the cooler. He jerked his head toward a small door and I followed.

In the storage room the cases of beer were stacked four, five, and six high next to the block walls and in the center of the room. We sat on cases and popped two fresh beers. Mister Alcie was wiry and sat lightly. His sport shirt with short sleeves needed tucking in. "I stayed in the South Pacific for three years," he said in his nasal drawl. "There were two hundred and fifty-six men in my company when we left San Diego. Six of us came back. I never did understand it."

I half-smiled and sipped my beer. "You seen Earl?"

"Yeah. He's a real live big-city lawyer now." He swirled beer in his mouth and swallowed. "You knew he declared himself a conscientious objector, didn't you?"

"No."

"I thought you knew."

"No."

"He was able to finish law school that way." He looked me in the eye. "They went after him and told him he had to go. He told 'em he wasn't gonna do it. Just like his daddy. They took part of his daddy's brain out."

"Who?"

"The state. He refused to fight. Told 'em he wouldn't be a part of it. That's when everybody was rushing to join up, early in forty-two. Buck Winston got drafted and told 'em he just wasn't gonna do it. They put him on 'alternate service.' "

We got fresh beers.

Mister Alcie continued. "We were shipping out at San Diego. The War Department pressed all the ocean liners into service, hauling people to staging areas. I was just a private and reported aboard this big fancy liner. They had it converted for hauling troops, and we had to wait in line to get our quarters assignments. Everybody else was getting sent to wards where they slept six deep and got showers every third day, but by my name it said 'Report to 0-3 deck steward,' and the steward was Buck Winston. That was his alternate service. He put me in a stateroom by myself. There were generals on that ship who didn't have it as good as I did. Buck would slip up there every night, and I'd invite some buddies from boot camp, and we'd play poker all night. We didn't give a shit. Didn't bother us he'd took the job on the ship. Everybody was doing something. Didn't really matter who did what. They found out he'd been running the poker game. It pissed them off. They sent him to a hospital in Philadelphia. The doctors there said he was crazy, said he had a bad disorder, and they sent him to the state hospital. They took out part of his brain. He still stays on the ol' Hainted Place, on the south side of the road, beside the store."

"I always thought he was just crazy," I said. "I didn't know they took part of his brain out. Earl didn't ever say anything about it."

"Wasn't long after he had that operation, I got home from the war, and Buck came by the house one night. I was staying back here at the home place with my momma and daddy. Buck said he had just fell in love. He went in the back to the new bathroom and took a shower. Put on some work clothes of mine, said they were

clean and his weren't. He borrowed ten bucks. Borrowed my car
with a full tank of gas. It was a thirty-eight Ford, had a six-cylinder
engine. It ran good. I gave him a blanket and a case of beer. The
next day my car smelled like raw bacon and fish, sitting out there
in the sun with the windows up. The gas tank was empty, the beer
was gone, my clothes were filthy. That's where Earl came from.
His momma took off after he was born. Buck raised Earl, but Buck
just don't think about what he's doing. He can't. They took out part
of his brain."

"What'd they do to Earl?"

"Nothing."

We sat for a moment drinking our beer.

I said, "I want to buy some land."

"Got any money?"

"I saved some while I was gone."

"How much land ya want?"

"As much as I can get."

"Land's getting tight."

"You got any you'll sell?"

"I ain't been looking to sell any."

"You got any land you'll sell me?"

Mister Alcie drank some beer. "They been talking about a new
Sunday-school building over at the church. I've been thinking
about paying for it if they'll name it after my momma and daddy.
The ol' Hainted Place is eighty acres."

"How much?"

"They need thirty thousand to build the building. You gotta let
Buck Winston keep living in the house and running the store. I
don't charge him any rent. He sells a little food, a little gas. I keep
it stocked for him. All the open land's planted in early beans. I'll
get my beans out by fall."

"Do you want cash?"

"You got cash?"

"I haven't spent any money in the last year, and they paid me
a lot."

"Just give the money to the church. Tell 'em it's in honor of my momma and my daddy."

When Mister Alcie Pace told me which land he would sell, I knew all the trees, where all the old gullies were, where the topsoil was thickest and where there was no topsoil, and where there was surface rock. It was the piece of land I wanted out of all the pieces of land I knew, and I knew all the land, because in Hepzebiah Community the preacher and his family went to a different home every Sunday, after church, and after we ate a big Sunday dinner Beth and I would go out to play, sometimes with children from the family we were eating with, while the grown-ups sat at the dinner table and talked. We would wander through all the woods around the place we were visiting, and after visiting a lot of places we ran into familiar woods and began to understand how all the land fit together, and we knew where the property lines ran and who owned what, and we knew where the roads and streams cut across people's land.

The Hainted Place had been part of the Harteezy plantation until Colonel Harteezy came home from the war and gave eighty acres to Uncle Goody's granddaddy when the colonel set the slaves free. The land and single slave house were on a site the Indians had said was used for ceremonies. The Indians said it was a place for ceremonies because it is where lightning strikes. The slaves said the land was hainted. When Colonel Harteezy set Uncle Goody's granddaddy free, the colonel named the slave family the Hainteds, because the colonel did not want them to be Harteezys and because the eighty acres Colonel Harteezy gave Uncle Goody's granddaddy was called the Hainted Place.

The Hainted Place is split by the road that had been the main plantation road from the plantation house to the slave quarters. Slaves had driven the work wagons and runabouts through the creek at the only place the spoked wheels would not mire up, at the bedrock in the bottom. The road is perpendicular to the creek and splits the Hainted Place in half.

The forty acres to the north of the road is the high ground overlooking the bottom where Horse Creek flows north to south. The creek is named for the horse fish that come up from the river in the spring and spawn. The fish are big and have faces like horses, flared nostrils and wide eyes. The only people who catch and eat the horse fish are the black people, and they only do it when they are drunk from funerals and holidays. The fish are bony, like a chicken neck, and their meat tastes like mud.

Slaves built the shack on the Hainted Place, on the north side of the road, for the slave who made the whiskey and the music. It was the center of the plantation, halfway between the plantation house and the slave quarters. The slave who made the whiskey and the music never got along with the rest of the slaves and had to live apart.

Buck Winston lives in a shack to the south of the road. Buck's shack was built by one of the Harteezy boys before the war. The boy was killed at Bull Run, and after the war the house was used for Hainted family tenants and sharecroppers until all the topsoil washed into the bottom and the boll weevil came and Uncle Goody's people had to move to Detroit and get jobs doing public work. Uncle Goody was the only one who stayed, and he worked the land until his children were educated and left to get jobs; then he gave the old Hainted Place to Mister Alcie because Mister Alcie had been paying the taxes all those years and paying to educate all the black children, and Uncle Goody became the sexton at the church.

Mister Alcie likes to be the first in the community to have new things. When cinder blocks were new he built two stores, the one in front of his momma and daddy's, Mister Alcie's Place, and the one at the Hainted Place on the south side of the road, Buck's Place. Mister Alcie opens Mister Alcie's Place every day when he finishes his plowing, late in the afternoon. His farming comes first. Buck opens at five A.M. and closes after dinner so he can start watching TV. One of the two places is open at every reasonable hour to serve the community.

The woods on the Hainted Place are mostly pine and mixed hardwoods in volunteer stands that came after the pure hardwoods had been cut. The pines grow tall and produce good lumber, and they grow from a seedling to maturity in half the lifetime of a man. Parts of the creek bottom are so steep and rugged that no one has tried to cultivate them or live there, and there are pure hardwood stands, mostly beech. If nobody needed any more lumber, if the forests were left to spring forth and grow and die, if the natural order were allowed to rule, the beech trees would again dominate the woods, the fields in the bottom, and the places where the houses are.

I went back to the parsonage. We cooked steaks on the grill to go with fresh vegetables and pie. It was a celebration in subdued tones, the best effort of us all in the fashion we were used to. The words were passed around like the string beans, with each person taking a helping in turn. We all felt blessed, even before Daddy's long blessing. We sat talking at the picnic table behind the parsonage until the food was gone. It was early summer. Mosquitoes came with the dark. Some neighbors saw us in the yard and drove the short distance to visit. They got out of their car and saw me. Miss Nellie had a cake she had made and she hugged my neck. The sky cast a yellow hue just at dusk. The neighbors stared at me, into my eyes, as they said their hellos and welcome homes. They never stopped looking at me while they smiled and told me briefly about who was home from college for the summer and who was getting married. Then they said a quick goodbye. We watched them back into the dirt road, wave one more time, and creep in low gear to their house down the road. We all pitched in to clear the table and take the dishes inside. Before I took my load of dishes inside I scanned the tree line behind the cemetery. There was no movement.

THE CITY
JUNE 1971

Earl and I were called the "Star-Spangled Twins" in high school because we were excused from class ten minutes every morning and every afternoon to go outside and raise and lower the flag. He usually ran the rope-and-pulley operation and I hooked the flag up and made sure it didn't touch the ground, because if it touched the ground we would have to burn it. We worked the flag every school day for years, until we graduated, but we never hung around together.

Earl told me on the playground in the fifth grade that someday he would get off that Hainted Place and away from that store his daddy ran, away from working for Mister Alcie Pace, away from living on the big man's land. More than anything else he wanted to get away from the Hainted Place. And he told me he was going to marry Judy.

Judy made her choice early on. It was me. Earl stuck with her at school all the time and I hung back and watched. Then one day, after we had rung the bell in the seventh grade, I went to Judy and told her that I liked her. She said she had been hoping I would come to her and tell her that I liked her. She said Earl was always

117

talking. I told Judy I thought she was pretty. She told me she liked me. After class we would hide together in the halls at school during break, around corners in the shadows, hiding from Earl. He knew we were hiding together and he knew why we were hiding together. It never seemed to bother him.

Mister Alcie Pace told me I ought to go see Earl to make sure everybody understood about me owning the Hainted Place. I called Earl from the air base one weekend and Earl told me to come on up to the city to his place that night, there was going to be a party. He said we could talk about the Hainted Place.

There was some fog on the way to the city. It was already night when I left the air base. After I had driven for an hour I slowed for a curve, shifted to third, accelerated out of the turn, and speed-shifted to fourth. I whistled a few notes, turned on the AM radio and listened to the static, then twisted the dial until some scratchy country music started. I looked at the radio, the little green background light and "Conelrad" marked prominently on the dial, then back at the lonely road—and locked the brakes and went into a skid, grabbing third gear, then second; then I left the pavement, and when I stopped on the shoulder I let the engine idle and got out. I smelled burnt rubber.

"You sorry little son of a bitch! Get outa the middle of the goddamn road!"

The puppy sat and rubbed its tail on the pavement and stuck its tongue out and whimpered, shifting on its haunches.

I looked around at the woods and the fields. No houses. "Where'd you come from, anyhow?"

The puppy stood, then sat back down and whimpered.

"Did you come out of that soybean field?"

I walked to the puppy, knelt, and picked him up by the scruff of the neck. He was brown and white, with short hair, lots of extra skin, and big feet.

"You got spunk," I said. The puppy whimpered. "I'll call you Soybean." His belly was pink with black splotches. I walked to

James Louis, cuddling him. "Naw—I'll name you Soybean, I'll call you Bean." I put him on the front seat.

"Sit."

He balanced in a crouch, rocking with the motion of James Louis idling, crouching slightly.

"Sit."

He looked at me and cocked his head. At first his ears drooped like a hound's; then he lifted them erect, at attention.

"Sit." I grabbed his rear and mashed it down, onto the seat, and let go. He stood.

"Sit." I mashed him again and let go. He stood.

"Sit."

He looked at me with a blank stare, and waddled his rear, and sat. He sat for several minutes.

We drove through the flat farm country, past the crops and homes of the tenant farmers. There was a place I liked to stop when I drove from the air base to the city. When I slowed down to turn into the place, Bean stood on the seat. I allowed him to do it. The sign on top of a metal post was a blue neon bird with several pairs of neon wings. Day or night, every day of the year, the neon bird flapped its wings up and down, up and down. The bird's beak pointed to a pair of old gas pumps beside a country store, a wooden building with horizontal lap siding painted white, with ancient, faded Nehi, Lucky Strike, and Maola signs scattered around the outside and in the windows, and a Merita Bread screen door. Just inside was a hole in the oak floor, worn there by years of first steps.

When I entered the store some old codgers were sitting around a wood stove, watching.

"That dog out there in your car hunt?" The man had a squeaky voice.

I pulled my wallet and reached into my front pocket for change. "Ain't even growed good yet an' he'll run a deer, tree a squirrel or coon, run a rabbit in a perfect circle," I said. "An' he'll point an' fetch a bird, an' talk to a fox all day."

The old man looked outside, then at the others. I paid for some gas, then went outside and pumped it. I drove into the dusk and rubbed Bean's head. He curled beside me and slept on the seat until we got to the city.

I found Earl's apartment in the city and parked in a numbered space. I told Bean to stay and left the windows cracked so he could breathe. The buildings were a few years old. The construction was cheap brick and plywood, and you walked under metal stairs to get to front doors. I knocked, then tried to turn the knob; it was locked. Then it opened. Earl was taller and more slender than I remembered, with wire-rimmed glasses, and he smiled real big and stuck out his hand. His long, dark hair hung loosely over his ears.

I shook the hand and I looked into his eyes for a flash, then inspected the entranceway. "Nice place you got here," I said. Our hands dropped and Earl said, "Come on in." He backed into the room and turned and walked toward the kitchen. "Want a beer?" The apartment was painted sheetrock. The room was scattered with cheap furniture and a few plants and pillows.

"You ever seen me turn one down?"

Earl laughed his shrill, hacking laugh, like a hyena's, and said, "Not yet." He brought out two beers and gave one to me. We popped the tops and drank, and as we swallowed we both looked around the room. "This party's a bunch of young lawyers I've met." He was fidgeting, putting his hands in his pockets, shifting his weight from foot to foot, crossing his arms. "A few accountants, a couple of judges, professional people. Good crowd. It's just a blowout, no special occasion. There's so much pressure in professional life! I didn't know that until recently, and they don't teach it in law school." He smiled. "Somebody has a party every weekend. We enjoy asking other people we know. Sorta mix it up. Makes for good parties. Thought you might enjoy it."

"Looks like a nice place. Found me a place off base, on the water. Got a dog."

"Are you going back over there?"

"I don't think so. . . . Who's still around? You seen anybody?"

Earl sipped his beer and shifted his weight to the other foot and looked at, stared at, an abstract print that was hung from an eight-penny finishing nail on the wall. "Let's see . . . ah . . . Rodney and Stella got married . . . did you know that?"

"Yeah. Beth wrote me about that."

"Saw Joe when he got home. He's fucked up, you know? Got back from Vietnam six months ago. He was a cook. You know that? Sat on his ass cooking."

"He went."

Earl smiled, showing his tobacco-stained teeth. "Saw Margaret the other day. Oh, yeah! You ought to see Judy! You talk about somebody who blossomed! Beautiful tits—she's got an ass like a forty-dollar mule!"

"Maybe I'll go see her."

"I've been going out with her."

I smiled.

"So you bought the Hainted Place. Blood money goes a long way, doesn't it?"

"Do you think what I've been doing was wrong?"

"Yes, I do."

When I didn't answer, he said, "You gonna let my daddy stay and run the store?"

"He can stay as long as he wants to."

"You gonna build you a house?"

"Gonna fix up that old shack where Uncle Goody used to live."

"You're insane."

"Where's the party?"

"We can walk."

"I thought the party was at your house."

"It's at the judge's house. We can walk."

"Gonna be anything there to fuck?"

"Not for you."

We walked through the night air, across a new street, past

small houses with decks and garages, all alike. We let ourselves into the house. People were scattered around in little groups, talking and laughing and drinking and smoking. Some of them glanced at me. A woman with fat thighs in britches and chopped bangs stared at my western shirt, Levi's, boots, shaven head. I felt naked. Some of the people spoke to Earl as he waved at them, smiling, and moved through the crowded room toward the kitchen. I followed, trying to be casual. Earl started talking to a middle-aged man. I kept moving. The music was loud.

There was very little room in the kitchen. The people who were walking in and out were in each other's way, saying "Excuse me!" and smiling at the ones they didn't know. Two women with good teeth and clear, clean complexions paused to trade comments or secrets or jokes. They smiled at me. I smiled back and worked my way through the people to the sink that was full of beer and ice, and popped a beer and turned to watch the people.

A woman walked toward me and looked me in the eye, then opened the refrigerator, bent forward, and moved her head around, looking. She had blond hair and green eyes, like an actress I had seen in a movie about a woman who lived in Naples. She had on a full skirt and a sleeveless, embroidered blouse that drooped when she bent forward, and no bra. Inside the blouse her breasts hung like perfect melons, and her nipples were like stems on the end.

"What are you looking for?" I asked.

"Beer. I thought I put it in the refrigerator."

"Somebody must have taken it out and put it in the sink."

She straightened up and closed the refrigerator door and looked in the sink.

"Most ladies don't like beer," I said.

She took a beer and stepped toward me. "I had a brother." She popped the top and took a sip, smiled, and said "Thanks."

We both looked around the kitchen and into the living room where more people were coming in and greeting their friends, and we sipped the beers.

She asked, "Army?" and when I told her Marine Corps she stopped. "My brother was in Charlie One-Seven during Tet," she said. "Did you just get back?"

"Yes."

We sipped the beers and looked around the room.

"Maybe you knew him," she said.

"I went in the Air Wing, lost contact with the ground people."

"We got a letter from his lieutenant."

"I'm sorry."

Two men pushed their way through the crowd, talking loud. They were wearing unbuttoned sports jackets, and their hair was over their ears to their shoulders, but neat. One grabbed the other's sleeve, trying to keep up. ". . . and they had just testified that the culverts were big enough to carry all that water. My client went by there right after the rain and had his camera with him and the pictures were lousy . . ."

The woman moved toward me and our arms touched. I backed into the corner where the counter was covered with hors d'oeuvres, and the two men smiled at us and spoke to each other in normal voices.

"Want a drink?"

"Yeah—doesn't matter what kind. . . . Anyhow, the pictures were lousy, but they showed the water backed up just before the road washed out, and they didn't know we had the pictures."

We were side by side, drinking beer. The two men ate some of the pieces of meat and cheese.

"So they made a motion to dismiss the evidence, and ol' Judge Poole says forget it and gave us damages plus twenty grand for breach of contract."

"I love that kind."

"No kidding! But I've got one coming up . . ."

The woman spoke to me. "You want to go to the patio?"

I nodded and we started out of the kitchen. The two men kept talking and moved toward the food and looked at me when I worked my way past them. As we went through the living room we passed a group of men and women who were laughing and talking and passing a joint around. The patio was on the other side of two sliding glass doors, and beside the doors, next to the wall, were two men making a new hundred-dollar bill into a tight roll, talking quietly over lines of coke on a wooden tea cart.

I slid the door open and the woman walked out and I followed her. I looked back into the room as I closed the door. People were having conversations in small crowds. As new people came, the crowds flowed and changed. The voices blended into a low roar. Rock music was making the little needles on a new sound system bounce up and down. Most of the noise stayed inside when I closed the door. Earl was watching from inside with a blank stare that I returned through the glass.

"During the day they put other people in jail for what they do at night," she said. "I can't believe I'm a part of it."

Somebody increased the volume on the stereo, and the people talked louder so they could hear each other over the noise of the music.

I asked, "What are you doing here?"

"I married one of them. We were in college and he was handsome, and in a fraternity, and wanted to be a lawyer. He wanted to make the world better, protect the innocent, so everybody could live in peace." They were becoming more animated and talking more directly to each other.

I turned away from the people and the sliding glass toward the parking lot and the few stars that were visible through the glare of the city. "Is this whole city like this?" The glare reflected high into the sky.

"My brother's things are in the garage," she said.

I followed her there. New tools hung on an unfinished wall. Old furniture was stacked with junk in a U-shaped pile. Oil spots had stained the concrete floor. She switched on a bare bulb and took a briefcase out of the bottom of an antique cupboard and scattered the contents on a work table.

"Corporal stripes. . . . Bronze star with a 'V' for combat service," I said.

She lit a cigarette and walked around the room, slowly, listening to what I had to say.

"Basic orders to WestPac—the Western Pacific. Citation for a Purple Heart."

"I thought that was for being injured."

"He qualified."

She bit her lip. "These goddamn people." She threw the cigarette on the floor and turned away from me. She leaned her forehead against the wall and rocked slightly. I went toward her.

"I'm sorry your brother got blown away."

She turned back to me. The door from the outside opened and one of the men from the party walked in and stopped. He looked at me and the woman, then walked toward the cupboard.

"Excuse me. Got to get more whiskey," he said. "I'll just be a second." He got the whiskey and left.

The woman went to an old framed mirror and wiped her face and straightened her hair. "We'd better go."

We walked around the outside, stepping through shrubbery; she opened the sliding glass door and went into the room. I stayed on the patio, took a wad of tobacco out of my back pocket, bit a chunk, and started working up a plug. The people in the room watched the woman as she got a beer, popped the top and drank. Earl came onto the patio and closed the door behind him.

"Don't mess with the judge's wife."

"When you become a lawyer do you automatically know things? I thought you boys based your questions on facts you can prove."

"The judge asked me if that skin-headed son of a bitch messing with his wife was a friend of mine."

"Did you tell him no?"

"I have to practice in his court. I told you there was nothing here for you."

"We had a nice talk."

"Don't try to fuck the judge's wife."

"We both got something out of the talk."

"He's a judge."

"Do judges know what's right?"

"This is the judge's house! Don't mess with his wife."

Bean was in James Louis and glad to see me. I was glad to get back to something familiar. Bean had peed on the floor and shit on the seat. I took him out of the car and rubbed the shit on his face and beat him. The drive back to the air base was six beers' worth. Bean squalled for a while, then whimpered, then slept. I decided I would find Judy and tell her I had bought the Hainted Place. I knew she liked the place. She might like to go out there with me, maybe for a picnic.

After an hour on the road and my first three beers I had to pee and stopped at the gas pumps by the bird with the flappy wings. Bean woke and stood on the seat. I got out. A little old man came out of the store, then went back and hollered, "He's out here right now!"

A dozen old codgers came out in single file. I watched them gather in a semicircle around the pumps and the back of the car while I pumped gas.

"That's him?"

The old man said, "Yep! That's him."

"He don't look like he could run a deer."

All eyes were on Bean, who was looking from face to face, his head held high, his tail pointed straight backwards, standing on the seat.

"If'n he kin run a rabbit, he kin run a damn deer."

A man by the pumps said, "Well, he ain't worth no goddamn five hundred dollars. I can tell ya that right now."

I walked into the station, listening to the banter.

"Shit! I'd give five hundred dollars jus' for the coon dog in 'im."

"You're crazy as hell, Roland. That dog ain't stout enough t' whip a coon."

"Look at him! That's a *smart* dog! He don't have t' whip a coon. He'd outsmart him."

I waited inside for the old man, gave him the right change. When I returned to the outside, one of the old codgers spoke. "Ya take five hundred dollars for that dog, mister?"

I looked at the men, glancing from face to face. "The dog's not for sale. Sit." Bean sat, his head still held high, and watched the men watch him.

CHERRY POINT
JULY 1971

The hangar deck was swept clean. All the airplanes and equipment were outside, on the line, where a formation of nimbus clouds was pumping a light spring shower across the base. The enlisted men were at ease in their formation, dressed in pressed uniforms. I joined the other officers who were milling around at the end of the enlisted formation. All the flags were in place.

When the band started playing, the sound they made was dominated by the dull thuds of the drum. As the men played music the people in the hangar walked smartly to their places, readying for the ceremony. The crisp music and the bootsteps of the color guard marching to their place echoed in the empty hangar.

The band stopped. The adjutant's command voice started the ceremony. The officers-in-charge called their people to attention and then parade rest. The band played again. The squadron commander trooped the line, then went to the center of the formation, facing it. The adjutant stood by the commander's side and called the squadron to attention. Then he called, "Officer to be decorated! Center, march!"

I stepped from my position and marched to the center of the

formation, to my place one pace in front of the commander. We saluted. The adjutant read from a book:

> "The President of the United States takes pleasure
> in presenting the Distinguished Flying Cross
> to Captain Horace A. Hardy, Junior,
> United States Marine Corps,

The commander and I were at attention, face to face, two feet apart. I had just met him. He was my new commander. It was my first day at the squadron. At first I could not decide whether to look at the bridge of the man's nose or his eyes. I settled on the nose. There was a small wart in the crook of his eye. The commander seemed to be concentrating on my chin.

> "for heroism and extraordinary achievement in aerial flight
> while serving as a pilot with Marine Attack Squadron 225,
> Marine Air Group Eleven, First Marine Aircraft Wing,
> in connection with combat operations against the enemy
> in the Republic of Vietnam.
> On the night of 13 December 1970,
> Captain Hardy launched from the Da Nang Air Base
> as pilot of an A4E Skyhawk aircraft
> assigned an armed reconnaissance mission
> along a heavily defended supply route
> deep in enemy territory.

I wiggled my knees slightly and scrunched the cheeks of my ass together because that's what my drill instructor had taught me to do while standing at attention.

> "Arriving over the designated area,
> he established contact
> with the forward air controller (airborne)
> and was assigned to attack enemy trucks

moving along the supply route.
Undaunted by the intensity of the hostile fire
directed at his aircraft and the difficulty of maneuvering
his Skyhawk over the rugged terrain
in the darkness
in adverse weather conditions,
Captain Hardy skillfully executed a rocket attack
and delivered his ordnance with such pinpoint accuracy
that three large secondary explosions were observed
when three of the trucks were destroyed.

I looked at the commander's left eye, at the wart. The men in
the formation were standing at parade rest, sweating in the muggy
heat. The adjutant's command voice was beginning to crack. The
commander was looking into my eyes, one at a time, back and
forth. I picked up the pattern and switched eyes every time he did.

"Seeking a target for his remaining ordnance,
he soon located other vehicles moving along the road and,
despite a solid overcast
and the heavy volume of enemy antiaircraft fire,
delivered the remaining ordnance on the moving target.
Captain Hardy's courage, superior airmanship,
and unwavering devotion to duty
in the face of great personal danger
were instrumental in accomplishing
the hazardous mission
and were in keeping with the highest traditions
of the Marine Corps
and the United States Naval Service.
For the President,
William K. Jones,
Lieutenant General,
United States Marine Corps,
Commanding General,

Fleet Marine Force,
Pacific."

The hangar was quiet. The commander took the medal from the adjutant, fumbled with the clasp, and pinned the medal on my uniform pocket. He fumbled with the clasp some more before getting the medal like he wanted it; then he took the citation from the adjutant and handed it to me with his left hand. We shook right hands. The commander mumbled, "Congratulations, Captain. You should be proud. I am designating you the squadron test pilot."

The bird had just been overhauled. They needed somebody to fly it before somebody else could fly it. That was my job. Fly those birds before the new guys get in them. Make sure they are safe.

I took my usual shots of Jack Daniel's and suited up for the test. The one thing I always loved to do was fly those airplanes the way they were designed to be flown. I always wanted to make them do all they could do.

I leveled at twenty thousand feet over the ocean and went through the engine tests. Slow flight. Stalls. High G turns. Negative Gs. Then I pushed the nose into a thirty-degree dive toward the ocean, picked up point-eight-five Mach and executed an Immelmann, a split S from thirty thousand feet into a loop, then a full cloverleaf to a Chinese Immelmann. Seven minutes of constant Gs. That left me at twenty-eight thousand feet sitting almost still. I could see my reflection in the canopy mirror against the brilliant, clear sky. All the colors were pure. There were no shadows. I could have been anybody there in the cockpit. I could have been nobody, just a pile of flight equipment, helmet with visor down, gloves and survival gear and speed jeans. There was no skin showing. The pile of flight equipment that was me was not moving.

I rolled inverted and pulled through to a split S to the deck, fifty feet above the water at five hundred knots, pointed toward land.

I went feet dry and flew straight, down low, for fifteen minutes, a hundred and fifty miles, clipping the tops of trees. The people along roads and working in fields and on streets in towns looked up, horrified. Point-nine-four Mach. The city popped out of the trees and began to rise on the horizon. I pulled the master arm out of its detent and set it in the on position. "Low angle. Lay down. Nape and snake. What a target." The buildings downtown were getting bigger. I turned quickly, stayed near the tops of the trees. I spotted a railroad track. I flew down the track, barely missing the telegraph poles. Everything close was fast motion, the poles came at a regular clip. The distance appeared, then immediately came close fast, but there were no more good targets. I switched the master arm to off. A water tank appeared with PIEDMONT painted on its side. At the last possible instant before hitting the tank I rammed the stick into my crotch, waited until the airplane was perfectly vertical. I looked up for Pete. I pegged the stick to the right, completing a turn on the roll axis every two seconds. At thirty-two thousand feet I gave out of airspeed and leveled off and pointed toward the coast, descending so when I got there, back over the ocean, I was level and fast and low.

I pushed the throttle forward, setting the engine on ninety-eight percent, and dropped the nose and leveled a hundred feet above the ocean. The bird was slick with nothing hanging underneath to create drag and slow me. I picked up speed running parallel to the beach, then nudged the nose forward until I was skimming the water, just above the tops of the waves, roostertailing, the blast of the airplane sucking the water in a plume behind me. Ahead the swales and whitecaps, blowing spray, moved under my airplane like mountain peaks.

The blast was deafening. The airplane shook with a sharp thud. I eased back on the stick and the throttle. The engine fire light came on. Four hundred feet, four hundred knots. The RPM on the engine was winding down. Eight hundred feet. I was climbing four thousand feet per minute trading airspeed for altitude. I smelled the smoke, acrid and piercing. At fourteen hundred feet the airspeed was two hundred and twenty knots and the hydraulic system failed. I tried to maneuver the stick, then put my right hand on the "D" ring between my legs, and I jerked straight up.

The glass on the canopy shattered and I was tumbling end over end. The chute popped and the harness straps squeezed my nuts. I looked toward the ocean—*don't look down*—then crossed my legs and grabbed a riser in each hand, looking straight ahead, drifting backwards in the wind. My feet hit the water and I was thrown under the surface on my back. The water made my gear heavy. I swallowed water and fought to get to air; I thought I almost died. I wondered why since I was good. I released the parachute and inflated the life jacket, and pulled the survival pack toward me and swallowed several more gulps of sea water before I could get the small raft inflated. I was coughing and gasping. I didn't want to get hurt. I wanted to get out of the raft and into the trees where I could hide.

When I got into the breakers several men swam out from the beach and pulled me onto the sand. There were hundreds of people standing in small groups, in their bathing suits and hats and sunglasses, watching. Some of the children wanted to touch me.

I entered the group commander's office and stopped in front of the desk and faced John Rossi. "Captain Hardy, sir."

"You okay?"

"Back's kinda sore." I stood at attention.

John Rossi exhaled and leaned back in his chair. "What happened?"

"I was running on the deck. Got a compressor stall. Zoomed. Got a fire light, secured the engine. Lost hydraulics. Ran outa airspeed. Punched."

"What were you doing on the deck?"

"Enjoying the ride, sir."

"Some free-lance photographer was on the beach and caught

the whole show on film. He sold a shot to a wire service. You're going to be on the front page of every daily in the country."

"The airplane caught on fire, Skipper."

"Why did it have to catch on fire in front of ten thousand goddamn taxpayers? Why couldn't you do it gracefully, at twenty thousand feet, where nobody could take a picture of it? A congressman has called the general wanting to know why you were showing your ass in front of all those tourists on the beach. We got a call from Piedmont—little town west of here? Something about a 'jet' breaking store windows? We just spent two million dollars rebuilding that airplane and it's sitting out there under two hundred feet of salt water. You think the general's proud of you?"

"Why's the general got a hard-on for me?"

"You broke an airplane, Truck! You screwed up. How close were you to the water?"

"Maybe ten feet. The engine blew, Skipper."

"How do you know you didn't ingest some spray? Ten fucking feet. You drinking this morning?"

"Yes, sir."

He looked out the window at the squadron hangar, the flight line with the airplanes in rows, the tower painted in red and white squares. "You didn't have enough foresight to leave the wreckage where we can get to it."

"All right, Skipper. I screwed up."

"I'll have to write a reprimand, put it in your record."

"My drill instructor, Sergeant Servantes, taught me that if you bust your ass and do the best you can in the Marine Corps, if you do better than everybody else, you advance in this outfit. You've flown on my wing, Skipper—you've seen me work. You know I'm good."

"You're a natural, Truck. This is what you are. But you've got to quit buzzing the natives."

"I'm not sure I want to fly anymore, sir."

"Your career will hold. I'll make sure of it. You'll get promoted."

"It's time to get out. I scared the shit out of me today."

"What can you do besides drive airplanes?"

"I've got a little piece of land up near Piedmont, a little place to live. I'll borrow some money and start farming. There's a lady I went to school with. I keep thinking about her. I might marry her."

"There's no carryover value into civilian life. You don't go from being a jet airplane driver to being anything else." Colonel Rossi looked at me.

"It's time, sir."

"I'm glad you got out okay," Colonel Rossi said.

I had to fill out forms because of the crash. At the bottom of the steps, bolted on a cinder-block wall, was a glass-cased bulletin board with pictures of the group chain of command. Colonel Rossi's picture was at the bottom, on one side of the board, beneath his superiors—generals, then civilians, then the President's picture was on top. On the other side of the bulletin board Colonel Rossi's picture was at the top, with pictures of his staff and squadron commanders in lines beneath him. All the photographs were 8-by-10 glossy black-and-white. I was not on there yet because I was new.

I went to the squadron and took off the gritty, damp flight suit. My balls still hurt from where those risers snapped tight when that chute popped. I put on my uniform and talked to the men who wanted to know if I was hurt and what it was like. Then I got into James Louis and waited in slow traffic until I got to the gate. Once off the base, I reached into the ashtray where I kept the neatly rolled joints and I smoked one, inhaling it as deep as I could. The sun was blazing through the salty, windy air. There was a crust of stuff on all my exposed skin. The heat of the afternoon was oppressive; it slowed the body to a crawl. I took seven months to get a mile. The music on the radio was hard country, bluegrass. Jimmy Rodgers, Bill Monroe.

There is the bridge! It was a big bridge. Sometimes the bridge did not sit straight with the road. Sometimes it was perpendicular to the road so big boats could go by in the water. *Which way is the bridge?*

There was a pair of hands working the steering wheel and the gears, and a pair of feet working the gas, brake, and clutch. I wanted the hands and feet to know which way the bridge was pointed, but I couldn't figure it out. So I let the hands and feet drive me home. They stopped at all the stop lights. They observed the speed limits. They always signaled before they turned, and they put the sun visor down to shade my eyes. Man! That son of a bitch was on fire. I could have smashed my head.

The trees were brilliant green and they all had limbs, and there were leaves or needles on the limbs. The smell of the salty, orange, brackish water was forced on me through the open window. The water was in the estuary where the shellfish grew big and clean, then stunk when they died and their shells split open and got full of black gloop. And everything was going by so fast! And it was so *pretty* . . . but you had to try to freeze a frame every now and then so you could have time to interpret what *it* was. There was a . . . *what was that thing?*

The nasal country whining started; then there was an electric guitar solo that led back into a duet where a man and a woman had been in love and now couldn't get along. The trees were singing, too, keeping time to the music, and James Louis shook each time the drum beat.

We turned onto a narrow dirt path and went a half-mile through the woods. The house was small and made of weathered juniper. It had a large chimney and windows across the side that faced the water where a single piling stood by itself in the shallows, except for a seagull on top, preening. The tide was in, and other gulls were skimming the smooth water searching for supper. There was no wind, and the marsh grass at the edge of the estuary was tall.

The hands and feet drove to a place near the house and stopped. Bean stood near the woods, going through his stretch routine. The left hand opened the door and I got out of the car. Bean's head was down as he walked toward me.

"Hello, General Bean. How are you, sir?" I saluted.

Bean looked at me weird. I bent over. The right hand rubbed his head. We walked toward the water where the tide was in. I took off the uniform except for the green jungle skivvies and waded into the shallow estuary. Bean swam beside me.

"We need us a boat, Bean Dog."

I went back to the muddy bank and sat in the black mess where the crabs had made holes and the marsh grass roots stuck out. Bean followed me out and did his dog-shake, sling-the-water trick.

"If we had us a boat we could go somewhere."

Then we went inside. I put some soup on the stove to heat and turned on the radio and lit another joint. The only light in the room was the faint light from outside, from the dusk. I took a puff, inhaled, exhaled, and opened a beer. I sat in a rocker. The room was big. The space between pictures on the wall was empty, stark, a void. One of the pictures was an ox pulling a plow. It was a wood carving, in blue. I looked back at the void, the empty space. Then I had to look away. I looked at the picture. A man was holding the reins that were attached to the collar on the animal. The man's face was strained. The animal was leaning into the collar, his muscles taut. The plow was making a small furrow.

There was a guitar solo. It was good stuff, funky rock and roll. I took a puff. The smoke crawled through my throat, going places. It smelled good, like alfalfa. The room was beautiful in the dying light, and I was sitting on the stage with the band, playing lead guitar. I studied the blank spaces on the walls. We constructed every note, every sound, perfectly. The bass line dominated and I started humming the bass.

"*Boom . . . boom-boom . . . ba-boom . . .*" I sounded good.

Bean was on the hearth by the fireplace across the room from where I sat in the rocker. It was almost dark, no shadows, everything dull grey. The stove clicked as the soup heated. The music got soft and slow. Bean was asleep.

"*Boom . . . ba-boom . . .*" I hummed quietly and rubbed my face, and as my hand went across my chest I felt another joint in my pocket. I lit a match and held it to my face in the dark. Bean came off the hearth attacking, growling and tense and moving forward slightly, then skirting to the side, always facing me, barking. He was bent forward, and the hair on his back was standing up. His growls became wilder and his teeth showed. The fire on the match went out.

I reached for the lamp and he went for my arm but missed. I jumped to the floor and tensed on all fours and growled at him. He lunged for me but caught himself when I moved forward and snarled and showed my teeth. We could barely see and moved our eyes around to take advantage of the dim light. Our bodies were broadside to each other and our heads turned sideways as we growled and moved in a tight circle, within striking distance of each other.

"Bean." I spoke quietly, gently. The voice made him relax some and back away. He went to the middle of the room, still watching me, quiet now. I stood, watching him, and switched on the lamp. He went to the hearth and glanced at me and lay down. "I almost killed myself today." He lay still and put his head on his feet.

I went to him and rubbed his head. "We're gonna get us a woman," I told him. "Old Judy. I told you about Judy. She's got great tits and an ass like a forty-dollar mule. We're gonna start farming."

HEPZEBIAH
OCTOBER 1971

Joe was so handsome he was almost pretty, like his daddy had been when he was young. Joe's daddy was still trim and muscular, like a gymnast. When we were in high school I liked to double-date with Joe because he looked like his daddy and could always get pretty girls to go with us who might not have seen me otherwise because I had acne and was skinny. We had played football and drunk our first beer and gone to church together.

I called Joe's house that Saturday morning and Joe's momma answered the phone. "Hello, Truck! My goodness! How have you been?"

"Pretty good."

"We haven't heard from you in a long time. Don't you ever get home?"

"Yes, ma'am."

"Are you still in the Air Force?"

"Marine Corps."

"That's right! Well, when do you think you might get home again?"

"I'm home now. I got out."

"Oh! Well, Joe called one day this week and said he might be home this weekend!"

"Yes, ma'am. I was calling to see if he was home yet."

"Oh! You knew he was coming?"

"Yes, ma'am. I called him earlier in the week."

"Did he tell you when he'd be here? He never tells me *when*, just that he might come."

"He told me late morning."

"Well . . . I went ahead and cooked. Why don't you come eat dinner with us?"

"My momma cooks for me."

"How is your momma?"

"Fine."

"You want me to tell Joe to call you when he comes?"

"Yes, ma'am."

"You save some room. I made a coconut pie."

"Momma did too."

"Well, you come on over any time you want to. I'm always glad to see my boys. You know, we've always thought of you as one of our boys."

"Okay. Thank you, ma'am."

Joe called after I had eaten the dinner Momma cooked, and I could barely move. "I got to get out and move around," Joe said, "ya know?"

"Me too. What do you want to do?"

"I gotta get some exercise. I ate four bowlsful of corn pudding. I musta ate a pound of corn pudding, ya know?"

"Why don't you ask your daddy if we can take some of his dogs out? They're bound to get tired of staying in those pens all the time. I bought the Hainted Place. We could go look around."

"I don't know. Daddy's kinda funny about his dogs."

"You get your daddy's dogs and we'll take some shotguns out to the Hainted Place and walk around."

Joe's daddy always had some real nice bird dogs. People used to fly in or come on the train or drive on the old two-lane roads so they

they could hunt behind Joe's daddy's bird dogs. They were mostly rugged men who liked to save money, and a few women who were hard but had some elegance about them. After each hunt they would arrange the breeding schedules and figure out who was going to get which puppies, and they drank whiskey until late in the night while me and Joe sat in the next room listening to them cuss and laugh.

Joe's momma and daddy lived in a big old frame home with a bachelor uncle, a widowed aunt, and Grandma Buckley. Out back was several acres, there on the edge of town, where Joe's daddy kept his garden and his dogs. The pens held little wooden houses covered by a tin-and-frame shelter. The rest of the area within the fences was walked-bare dirt.

We picked Lemon and Snow. They were both bitches and skinny, with squared-off faces and wide eyes. Snow was white except for some brown splotches that were strewn all over her, and Lemon was a pee yellow with white trim. They were both nervous and shaking as they got into the backseat of James Louis.

We started toward the country.

"Never heard much about you, Truck. Momma wrote me letters, told me you were flying."

"Yeah."

As I drove faster, out of town, I lit a smoke. The dogs in the back calmed, sitting on their haunches, looking out the windows at the fields which were brown from the early frosts and at the forests where the hardwoods were shedding their leaves. We turned onto the dirt road. Joe reached into the pocket of his field jacket and pulled out a flask, shiny beaten metal. He took a drink and passed it to me. I drank and passed him the smoke and slowed the Chevy at a small dirt path. Lemon and Snow stood in the backseat as we turned off the dirt road onto the path. I drove through puddles and past a hundred feet of thick pines and stopped in a field that was at least forty acres, starting off narrow, then getting wide, then narrowing again. Mister Alcie had harvested the early soybeans, leaving a six-inch stubble of stalks on the flat land.

I said, "Thought I'd go see Judy."

"I heard she's been seeing Earl."

"You ought not to say that. I might want to marry the girl."

"Have you talked to her?"

"No."

"She might be different. Maybe you ought to go see her."

"Maybe I will."

"You bought this place?"

"Mister Alcie let me have it."

"I had a bunch of money too. Pissed it away in Bangkok, ya know? You ever get a basket fuck?"

"No, but I heard about them."

We stopped in the edge of the bean field, got out, and opened the back doors. The dogs got out slowly, cautiously at first. Their noses immediately went to the ground. They started sniffing and running in small circles, keeping their noses right down close to the ground all the time; then they raised their heads and ran in opposite directions, one going to each side of the field.

Joe opened the trunk and we loaded the shotguns. "Daddy always wanted me to hunt with him, but I always just wanted to fart around like this, ya know?"

I looked around the edges of the field and saw only one dog. "Don't reckon they'll run off, do you?"

Joe shouted, "Come! Come! Here!" He pulled out the flask and motioned toward a big oak tree. We went over to it and sat on the roots that stuck out of the ground, holding our shotguns so they pointed up. I took the flask and a slug of whiskey and my eyes watered. I gave the flask to Joe.

"I told you about this place they sent me?" He took a drink. "There were these dogs there, ya know?" He drank again, then passed the flask.

Lemon and Snow came running and stopped and stared at us. They ran away sniffing the ground.

"There was wire an' mines around the base, but these three dogs somehow got on the base from a ville about a click down the road. They were all males. They were there when I got there, an' we called 'em Hero, Nero, an' Zero."

I laughed and looked down, almost choking, and shook my head and swallowed the hard whiskey.

"No shit! This is the truth! We called 'em Hero, Nero, an' Zero, an' they were like our pets—mascots, ya know? We fed 'em scraps from the chow hall. There was only about sixty of us there permanent, just the field kitchen an' artillery battery. The grunts would come through in their rotten boots, all glassy-eyed, an' rest up for a while an' catch a hot meal; then they'd go back out in the bush. We were always bored 'cause there wasn't anywhere for us t' go, so we fed the dogs. They followed us around when we went between buildings or had a work detail outside. All the grunts passin' through spoiled 'em, an' the old man, he didn't give a damn, he liked 'em too, an' he was the only officer there. Hero was big an' strong. And he was handsome, and flashy, ya know?"

"Yeah."

"He walked around like he owned the place." Joe smiled and leaned forward, scrunched down, and looked at me from under his hat. It was the hats that made us that day. His was a Greek fisherman's and mine was a black ten-gallon job. The sun was bright and the wind was brisk and gusty. Joe narrowed his eyes.

"We used to have a formation every morning before we turned to the day's work, an' old Hero would fall in line like the rest of us. So one mornin' we took him in the bunker an' got a pair of service-issue white skivvies with the hole for your pecker t' stick out of? . . . We put a pair of them on him backwards, so his tail stuck out the pecker hole? . . . An' we went out to the formation an' ol' Hero fell in line just like he was a private first class! When the ol' man saw him with that tail standing right up through that pecker hole, he cracked up . . . couldn't give the command for colors."

I scanned across the field at the tree line on the other side. "Where's the dogs?"

Joe stood and took a shot of whiskey from the flask and looked around the field. "Come!" he shouted. "Come! Heeaahh! . . . Hell, there she is, over yonder. She's pointin'! That crazy bitch found some birds!" He picked up his shotgun and started toward the open field. I followed him. It was a long hike, clear to the other side of the field and down about half the length. We didn't talk. The soybean stubble raked and scraped at the bottoms of our boots. The wind had almost died and the sun had broken through the clouds in places, shining in streaks. As we got closer to Lemon we saw Snow pointing too. They were frozen on the flanks of the best line of flight between the covey and the woods so if the birds wanted to flush and fly they had to come toward us.

We clicked the safeties off our shotguns and went into semicrouch position. The dogs were frozen, perfectly still in their points, and we were less than thirty yards from them, moving slow, when the rabbit jumped in front of us and ran straight toward the dogs.

I stood bolt upright and leveled the shotgun and fired. The covey of birds flushed in a whirl and the dogs broke point. I missed, and the rabbit turned broadside in a dead run when he saw the dogs headed for him. I broke the shotgun and was popping in a new shell when Joe unloaded. Joe's blast strung the rabbit out across several feet of sand and stubble, guts first, just as the dogs arrived and stopped, sniffing and snorting and prancing in their places. The red meat went unnoticed at first; then Lemon calmed and slowly turned her head toward the rabbit and sniffed. Snow ran ten feet and froze into a point toward the open field.

"I think you got him."

Joe laughed and pulled out the flask and removed the cap and took a drink of whiskey. "You ever seen such a long fuckin' rabbit? Must be five feet from his hind legs to his stomach!"

Lemon eased toward the carcass, which was mostly pinkish brown with dark areas and fur and some bones and blood. Snow held her point.

"Come! Come!" Joe took another drink and handed me the flask.

Snow came toward us, then joined Lemon in the slow sniffing around the rabbit.

"Let's drink some whiskey." Joe turned toward the car. "The dogs need to run around the field, find something to do."

We walked toward James Louis, dragging our feet in the bean stubble, breaking our shotguns, clearing the chambers. We had to walk across most of the cleared land. Evening had started. Long shadows were taking the field. The sun hit directly on some of the trees. They were yellowish green. We passed the flask and took long shots of the whiskey, wiping our mouths with the backs of our hands and saying "Ahhh . . ." when we finished each shot. The dogs were running and jumping and playing around, exploring; but I never saw either of the dogs eat any of the rabbit. We started the long hike toward James Louis with our shotguns broken and draped over our arms.

"Now Nero," Joe continued, "he had long, slick hair that stayed real neat, but he was always slippin' around hidin', an' he wouldn't let ya touch his head, an' he had a long nose an' beady eyes that were close together. We liked him because at night he walked around the base, all night. If anything came near the fence from outside he'd bark. Kind of a weird dog, ya know?"

"Yeah," I said. "Yeah."

"Most of Zero's teeth were gone an' he shook, but he wasn't old. He had lice, ticks, mites, mange, an' fleas, but he never scratched, an' flies buzzed around his head all the time. He smelled awful but was a real nice dog. Didn't shit where people walked or stick his nose in your crotch or bark. He was so awful lookin' that most people didn't have anything to do with him. I'd see him out behind the chow hall sometimes, lookin' scared half t' death an' hungry, an' I'd take some nice meat scraps to him, thinking it might help him grow some hair on the bare splotches of skin."

Lemon and Snow came running, tired, hassling. Shadows covered the field, making things dim. We all walked together to the car, Joe and I drinking from the flask. We put the dogs in the back. They flopped on the seat and stared out the windows as we drove out the path to the pavement and toward town.

"So we had these three dogs on this base, an' a bitch in heat slipped in from a gook ville down the road through the fence? When we saw her we knew all three of them dogs were gonna want t' fuck her. It was a question of who would go first. We all picked our favorites an' argued some about why one particular dog would deserve firsts. Then this ol' boy from Alabama said we should let Zero go first, 'cause if we didn't he'd be last, an' he's always last, an' how'd you like t' be last all the time? We figured he was right but we knew we'd have t' help him, 'cause he'd never hack it on his own.

"We put together one of those holdin' boxes out of orange crates an' wire an' some ripped strips of sheet, like I'd seen my daddy do when they wanted t' breed a bitch, an' we caught the bitch an' put her in there so she couldn't move. Hero was right there, sniffin' her ass an' tryin' t' mount her, an' we'd push him away. We were out on the back dock of the chow hall, across the parkin' lot from barrels of garbage, an' Nero was slippin' behind the barrels, hidin' and watchin'."

I slowed the car as we neared town. "Anything else in there?"

"Yeah." He handed me the flask. "Take the last swaller."

I turned it up and let the last drops drip on my tongue.

"It took a piece of cooked steak to lure Zero in close enough so we could get our hands on him, but we finally got a sheet over him—because nobody wanted to touch him—I mean, we're talkin' about a goddamn filthy dog, ya know?"

"Yeah."

"We picked him up with the sheet an' set him on that bitch's back. He caught her scent and his eyes got real wide, then he started humpin'. But he didn't know what was going on. The bitch started squallin' an' snortin' an' backin' up in that thing she was tied in. It was either the squallin' or the smell, but something got ol' Zero rolling. He started humpin' like crazy. Hero was tryin' to jump on the pile an' people were kickin' him away, an' Nero came out of hidin', howlin' like a wolf. Everybody on the base was there, all dirty in their jungle clothes. We had made bets on how long it would take, so most of us were checkin' our watches an' shoutin'.

Zero's head went up an' he humped harder—then his eyes rolled back so all you could see was white, an' he died! He fuckin' expired right there on that bitch's back!"

I turned into the driveway at Joe's house. "He *died*?"

"Graveyard dead."

Lemon and Snow stood in the back and started prancing, shifting their weight back and forth.

"Jesus!"

"Yeah, nobody'd figured he'd *die*, ya know? . . . Everybody wanted to collect the bets. While we were arguing, Hero ran into the crowd, looked around, an' he saw that bitch strapped in that thing, an' she was screamin' and scared to death. Hero ran to her an' knocked ol' Zero's carcass off her back an' laid a fuckin' on her. She screamed louder an' Hero just grinned—I swear his lips were drawn back so tight that his teeth were stickin' out an' he looked like he was grinnin'."

That's when I started laughing. We pulled behind Joe's house and got out of the car, laughing, bent over, both of us, and opened the back doors so the dogs could get out.

Joe's daddy had on rubber knee boots and tweeds and a heavy jacket. The squint lines on his face showed his age, and his tousled gray hair lay forward on his brow. He was toting two buckets of water toward the dog pens in the backyard when he stopped to watch us. Lemon and Snow ran to him, excited and animated. When he put the buckets of water down they slurped the water.

Joe's daddy shouted, "You water the dogs?"

Joe slammed the car door and answered, "We weren't near any water."

Joe's daddy walked toward us. His jacket was unfastened and hung open to both sides. The boots sounded hollow with each step. He stopped in front of Joe.

"You're drunk."

"I've seen you drunk."

"Not on a hunt."

"It wasn't a hunt. We went out for some exercise."

Joe's daddy turned and walked back to the buckets where the dogs were still drinking. He picked up the buckets and the dogs followed him toward the pen.

Joe and I went through the open back doorway into the house to a long hallway that was lit by a bare bulb centered in the high ceiling. The walls were pale yellow and had a wide baseboard, and there was a refrigerator in the hallway where a door opened into the kitchen. The house smelled like meat and pie. We stopped at the refrigerator and opened it and got two beers. We had our coats off and hung on nails when Joe's daddy came through the back doorway. At the same time Joe's momma came from the kitchen with her hands held up covered with flour.

"I thought I heard y'all come in. Supper'll be ready in twenty minutes. Can you stay, Truck?"

Before I could answer, Joe's daddy said, "Lemon and Snow are out there puking."

Joe's momma asked, "Truck, since you couldn't eat dinner with us, can't you stay for supper?"

Joe said, "Maybe they drank too much water."

"They're puking rabbit guts and fur. Did you shoot it?"

"Yes, sir."

I turned to Joe's momma. "No, ma'am. Momma will be waiting."

"I've told you never to drink when you're hunting, and I've told you never to let the dogs get near a fresh kill unless it's a bird."

Joe looked at me. He gave me a mock grin. Joe turned to his daddy and said, "They'll be okay."

"Lemon and Snow were my best dogs. You know when a good dog tastes red meat the dog goes to hell!" He was shouting. "They won't be okay! I'll have to give 'em away as pets! Goddamn useless dumbass!"

Joe leaped toward his daddy and swung hard and missed, and he went off balance. His daddy grabbed him from behind in a bear hug and wrestled him to the floor, landing on top of him, taking his wind, making him grunt.

"Joe! My God!" Joe's momma put her hands on her face and got

some flour in her hair and on her makeup. "What on earth . . .
Oh, my God! What's got *into* you?"

When Joe's daddy got Joe still, he looked at me and said, "Why
don't you wait outside?" Joe was grunting, trying to get free.

"Oh! What's he doing? Oh, my God!" Joe's momma clasped her
floured hands below her chin like she was praying.

The uncle appeared at the end of the hallway, and the grandma
leaned through the door from the kitchen, and they both stared.
I went outside. The dogs were barking. Joe and his daddy were
shouting at each other and grunting, and Joe's momma was
screaming.

I got into James Louis and revved the engine to three thousand.
Joe and I had fun when we were younger, before we both went
away. The mufflers sounded. I drove away from town. My water
temperature came up. I turned right onto Snakey Road and
stopped in the road. I checked the friction point on my clutch.
James Louis was tight. The autumn moon illuminated the
Headwaters in tones of grey. Snakey Road was three miles of
S-turns with a quarter-mile straightaway in the middle. You
stopped on the shoulder of the road at the beginning of the first
curve and sat in the dark alone; and you and your buddy had set
your watches so the second hands were exactly together; and you
waited. When the minute hand showed a minute to go, you pulled
out on the road and checked your gauges, and when the second
hand went straight up you burned rubber as far as you could burn
it and headed for the curves. They were banked wrong and had
bad shoulders and some were on hills, but you could not lose a
second because you had to hit the straightaway the same time
your buddy did, because he had started from the other end the
same time you had started from your end. If you did not meet him
in the straightaway you met him in a curve. And if you did it as fast
as it could be done, and he did too, you met your buddy on the
narrow bridge in the middle of the straightaway. You cut your
lights at the bridge so only the moon lit the scene of the bridge, the
trees, the creek, the empty road ahead, the curves in the dark.

I opened the ashtray and took out a joint and lit it.

"Never drove Snakey Road stoned." I talked to my car. "Charlie was cool. He smoked in front of his daddy and drank whiskey. Charlie's pants were pegged real tight. His hair was long and girls liked him."

I finished the joint and ate the roach and rammed the gear shift into first and gunned the engine. Rubber peeled off the rear tires with a great squalling sound. I went into the first curve accelerating.

James Louis was hugging the road and I was a part of the road. We were all singing the same song, in tune, going down the highway. We shot out of the last curve onto the straightaway. With the lights cut only the moon lit the scene of the bridge, the trees, the creek, and the empty road ahead. We crossed the bridge floating. The Chevy was wound out and stayed there until just before the first curve.

I cut the lights on and saw that we were going fast. I took all the curves on the inside, going slower. I passed the huge oak with the scab on the side of the trunk closest to the road where the bark had been ripped off when Charlie hit it. The tree had healed itself the best it could over time. I drove slowly. The massive trunk was solid. The scab was the size of the front end of a small car. The wood where the bark had been was weathered grey and bare. Charlie was gone and I knew I would never see Joe again. I shifted into second and accelerated.

"I'm gonna marry Judy," I told James Louis.

HEPZEBIAH
SEPTEMBER 1976–SEPTEMBER 1977

Sammy's Momma didn't have a name until Sammy was born. He was her first calf. She started losing weight when she got pregnant, but she stayed with the herd, working the pasture for several months. She gave up her status in the herd when her shit got watery, and she chose her corner of the pasture, a beaten-down bed of grass swamped by big, late-summer flies, and she got worse. I fed her every day, but she went down hard. Every day I worked her jaws for her so she could swallow food, and I stuck a Coke bottle down her throat, neck first, forcing water into her first stomach.

The day I called the vet I shoveled a pile of wet shit from behind where she was laying and washed her with a warm rag and some soap and water. I had never met the vet. I found him in the yellow pages.

The vet thanked me for washing her and turned to Sammy's Momma and examined her. He took his time. Some of the other cows came and milled around, chewing their cuds, getting up and down ass-first, moving slow. Sammy's Momma had chosen the low corner of the pasture. The cleared land inside the fence was knee-high in thick, late-summer grass that would be cut for hay after the first frost. Outside the fence was woods, thick under-growth, briars and honeysuckle, pigweed and vetch, kudzu and lespedeza. The other cows from the herd were in a ragged semi-circle around the square corner of the pasture where the open land was divided from the woods on two sides by the fence. The cows were curious. The vet's van was among the cows standing in the semicircle. The van was royal blue and trimmed all over in chrome, with chrome window vents and shaded windows, and it reflected the sunlight and the bright green of the pasture. It had a CB antenna. The vet had a full crop of black, wavy hair cut short. He had sharp angles in the bones of his cheeks. The cows turned their heads back and forth between the van and us in the corner and swished flies with their tails.

"You've got a pretty place," the vet said. He was wearing a shirt like a golfer would wear, with a little animal over his heart, and Army-surplus khaki pants and loafers. "Some people don't bother to keep their places up, but your place looks good." He was feeling Sammy's Momma's bones and muscles. He looked like he may have once been a salesman in a clothing store or a waiter in a good restaurant. He smiled all the time. "The calf's alive." A rubber glove covered his right arm all the way to the pit, and he stuck the arm up the cow to his elbow. Shit and blood were oozing out around where the gloved arm went in. Sammy's Momma was reduced to bones and skin covered with thick black hair, not the shape of a cow. Her eyes were wide and bugged out, causing her head to lose its shape. She let out a low moan that sounded like it was a long way away. "She's lost her muscles," he said. "Doesn't look like the infection's got to the calf." He was feeling around inside her, looking toward the van. "I've been wondering who lived here," he said. "I started to stop here going by one day last month."

"Is she gonna die?"

"She'll go into shock. As soon as you can see the calf you pull it, then call me. I'll give her something for her infection then. It's her only chance. You go down to Brach's Dairy and get some colostrum, get set up to feed the calf. It's a nice calf. You can save him, but she's lost her muscles."

He brought his arm out slowly, dragging the shit and blood in strands of thick, brown ooze. He pulled the glove off his arm, rolling the glove inside out. "You raised around here?" He was wiping his hands and arms with a bandanna.

"Been here all my life except when I was in the service."

"Is this your family place?"

"I bought it with the money I made in the war."

"You own the store too?"

"I own Buck Winston's store and that land across the road."

We walked toward the vet's van. I turned back for one more look at Sammy's Momma. She was on her side, breathing heavy, rocking in reaction to the breathing, wallowing in a loose pile like jelly in a bowl.

The vet said, "I've been looking for a place where I can do some experimental breeding with cows and hogs. I'll need enough land to raise hay and corn."

"Were you ever in the service?"

"I managed to avoid it." He looked around. "This is a nice place."

We walked up to the van. The cows scattered. Some bolted and some turned slowly and walked away. They went a short distance, then stopped and resumed their poses.

"Would you consider selling some of your place?"

"No."

"Who sold it to you?"

"Mister Alcie Pace."

"People tell me he doesn't sell land."

"He sells land to people he thinks ought to have it," I said, "and he gives the money to the church."

At the back of the vet's van was a dispenser that squirted Go-Jo when it was pushed. The vet pushed the lever with one hand while the other hand filled with white cream. He rubbed his hands together and wiped the cream up his arms, then scrubbed for a while, separating each finger on each hand for its own rubbing, looking toward Sammy's Momma in the corner of the pasture, and the cream became clear, then got cloudy as he rubbed; then the cream became foamy on his arms and hands, and the vet pulled a warm towel from a hamper and wiped his hands and arms clean.

"As soon as you can see the calf, you go ahead and pull him," he said. "Then call me right away, no matter what time it is. I want to work on that momma as soon as the calf's out." He said he was pleased to meet me and he left in the van.

I checked on Sammy's Momma several times during the rest of the day, in between jobs and chores around the place, and that night when Judy and I were ready for bed I slipped on some Levi's and my flight jacket with squadron patches all over it and my jungle hat and took a flashlight to the pasture to check one last time. Her eyes were bugged out farther and wandering and her gums were more grey than pink. The little white stubs that would become hooves on her calf were showing from her rear. I got the tractor with the flatbed trailer, some dressed lumber, and a come-along. Judy got up and put on jeans and a jacket and found some flashlights and we went to a stall in the barn. Judy set up the lights and spread clean wheat straw in the stall while I went to the bottom corner of the pasture with the tractor and trailer and put some ropes around Sammy's Momma. I hooked one end of the come-along to an elm tree and the other end of the come-along to the ropes around Sammy's Momma and ratcheted her up the dressed lumber until she slid onto the oak boards of the flatbed trailer, and I hauled her up the hill to the barn. The rest of the herd was not around. I backed the trailer into the barn so it was at the door to the stall. Judy held flashlights while I tried to lift Sammy's Momma off the trailer, but all I could do was roll her and ease her fall. Sammy's Momma tumbled down the dressed lumber into the middle of the stall. She was breathing and she groaned.

Three lights were hung on the bare boards of the stall, and Judy had two flashlights. I cut the tractor off, because the diesel smoke

was thick in the barn and starting to burn my eyes. The clean
wheat straw rustled when we moved. Sammy's Momma smelled
like diarrhea. I planted one flashlight so it would shine on her rear
and used my bandanna to wipe her. Judy was shining the other
flashlight on her. I pinched tight on one hoof with each of my
hands and braced myself against Sammy's Momma with my foot
and pulled and Sammy slid out like a drawer. His momma let out
a sigh. I pulled the membrane from his face and opened his mouth
with my hands, with one palm covering his nostrils. I blew into his
mouth, then released him and saw he was alive. He lay on his side
in the straw and his eyes were wide like he was scared and his
skinny legs twitched.

"Now I'm glad you left this building here," Judy said.

"Me too."

"But it looks so bad from the road."

"I'll paint it as soon as I get time."

"Sure."

"I'll put it on the list."

"You'll never do it, Truck."

"I'll do it."

"You can't even do what you're already doing. Is that calf going
to live?"

"I think so."

"That momma's dead. I don't think you've been doing this right,
Truck."

"I need to go call the vet."

"You should have called him sooner."

"He said to call him as soon as I pulled the calf."

"You ought to get another vet. Who is this fellow?"

"He's a nice fellow."

"He ought to be here now."

"I'm gonna go call him."

"I'm going back to bed. That cow looks like she's dead. How
much did she cost?"

"Two hundred dollars."

"How much will the vet charge to tell you she's dead?"

"I don't know."

I picked up the calf. "This is Sam," I announced. "For Uncle Sam. I'll call him Sammy."

"That's ridiculous," she said.

Sammy was moving and I put him in a corner of the stall in some clean straw.

"You're not in the Army anymore," Judy said.

"Marines."

"Why don't you forget about all that stuff?"

"I got to go call the vet."

I went to call the vet and Judy went back to bed, then I went to the stall to wait for the vet. When the vet came into the stall I was squatting down holding Sammy's head with one hand and forcing a plastic nipple into his mouth with the other. The lights were still hung. The colostrum I got from Brach's Dairy was oozing into Sammy's mouth, then dripping into the straw. Sammy had latched on to the nipple several times and sucked, and he had been able to swallow the milk. The best he could do in between the sucking was to lay still while I held the nipple in his mouth. I let the colostrum sift through, hoping he would start sucking again. His breathing was good.

The vet told me hello and took a quick look at Sammy without bending down, then he went to work on Sammy's Momma. He prepared three syringes, holding each one up to its opaque bottle and sucking liquid from them. He pulled her afterbirth and examined her inside, then gave her the three shots in her neck. He shot several blobs of paste from a tube into her throat and used the same Coke bottle I had been using to force water down her, and he massaged the muscles in her neck so she could swallow.

"You got a tarp?" He was kneeling, looking at his work.

"Got some tent tarp."

"We need to sling her. Got to make her stand. Her bones are

separated. We'll need tarp and some rope," he said. "And that come-along on the trailer out there. Has the calf swallowed anything?"

"He swallowed several times. Breathing's good."

"You ever slung a cow?"

"No."

"We'll put the tarp around her belly and tie the rope to the corners; then we'll hook the come-along over that rafter up there and hook the ropes to the other end of the come-along and jack her up, hang her by her belly so her feet are just touching the ground. Her head will sag way down, but she can breathe. If she lives, she'll get strong enough to put weight on her legs."

I helped him, and we slung Sammy's Momma like he said.

* * *

The house was as I had planned it. I had torn down the old part and built the new part. When I did it I knew nothing about building except that it could be done. I had put in the heat, the water, the electricity. I had made everything work right. It was where Wendy had been conceived on a cold night when my heart had leapt into my throat and stayed there for hours.

We were in bed and Judy was asleep. I couldn't sleep. I heard a cow lowing in the night. It was not one of my cows. I kissed Judy and got up and got dressed and went out to the pasture. I didn't tie my brogans and had only a T-shirt under my overalls. I put on the flight jacket and jungle hat I had taken to wearing whenever I went out. A wooden gate that I rarely used was broken in pieces on the ground, and Sammy was not in the pasture. The rest of my herd was still and settled below the pond. I heard the cow lowing across the forest again. She had come in heat and broken out from wherever she lived, probably Brach's Dairy, and wandered by our pasture and Sammy had broken out to follow her. It was his first time around a cow in heat since his piss thickened. She would wander as long as her heat lasted, then try to find her way home. Sammy would stay with her until she was out of heat.

I went in to tell Judy about Sammy being gone. She was awake. "I think it's time, Truck. I feel funny." She rubbed her belly. She was pudgy then; her thighs were big and had rolls in them, and her breasts were big and sagged, stretching the nipples and the brown circles around them. "I want to start the exercises. I think maybe it's time." Her crotch was almost hidden as she sat with her legs crossed Indian-style under her big belly. The skin on her belly was tight and smooth.

I told her what I thought had happened to Sammy and helped her lay on her back. I started counting to help her get her breathing cycle down. We had practiced so much, every night for a long time, and it still felt like practicing, but knowing it was the real thing made us practice like it was the real thing, like it was important. I told her Sammy would come back once the cow he followed went out of heat and found her way back home, because I thought the cow had come from Brach's Dairy and Sammy would be sure to find his way back to our place from there. I told Judy he might be able to hear me call in the mornings if it was cool and the wind was toward the dairy. She didn't start crying but tears trickled on her cheeks, and she had goose bumps, so I put her robe around her while she breathed.

I counted, "One, two, three, exhale."

"I hope Sammy's okay."

She grunted and struggled as I helped her with the robe, her belly was so big.

The baby was ready to come. We knew what to do because we had practiced so often in a group in the city and together at home, and we had things packed and ready. We had a checklist, and while Judy breathed and counted time between contractions I went through the checklist. Then I went outside and brought James Louis around and let him idle in the front drive. I left the parking lights on because it was so dark. The moon was not up yet.

It was after a full moon, and each night the moon came later and got smaller.

James Louis was warm when we got in and buckled our seat belts, hers loose above her belly. Our cows were below the pond, where they were every night before midnight.

Judy asked, "Where do you think that cow will go?"

"The one Sammy's chasing?"

"You think it's just one?"

"Could be more than one."

"Where will they go?"

"There's still plenty of wild grass in the bottoms. No frost yet. They'll go off and find a nice bottom and breed."

"I think you should find Sammy and bring him back," she said. She looked at me. "If we have a boy I want to name him Sam," she said. "Sam Hardy."

I told her as soon as she and the baby were okay and resting I would find Sammy and bring him back and make sure he was okay. I drove James Louis hard on the back road. We had all the windows up and the engine was running smooth on Snakey Road. Judy was breathing heavy. I was helping her count and I was watching, driving fast as I could to get to the new highway where I could make some time. She smiled and said "Uh-oh." She started moving in the seat. "I just peed on the seat." She felt her crotch. "It's my water still coming out."

We crested a hill. In the bottom ahead was a police car with a blue light that flashed one big time and one little time, then a big time again. I slacked off the accelerator and hit the brakes and saw an old Ford station wagon with the front smashed in and several black people and a dead black bull, and I pulled onto the shoulder past the wreck and stopped and got out. Judy was counting and breathing and looking at her watch and I told her it would not take long, that I would be right back, and she wanted to know if it was Sammy. I told her I thought it was Sammy.

The policeman was glad to know who owned the bull and

wanted to know if I had insurance because there was no insurance on the car that hit the bull. I told him we were on the way to the hospital to have a baby. He walked to James Louis in the flashing blue light and said something about how pretty fifty-five Chevys were and looked in at Judy. She was breathing hard, counting out loud, looking at her watch. Her housecoat was pink and her hair was tangled and oily; it needed washing.

"You okay?" he asked her.

"I hope none of those people were hurt."

"Just a carload of drunk niggers." He looked at me. "You ever say whether you got insurance or not?"

"Is the bull dead?" I asked.

"I shot him. He was busted all up and bellowing. Had some bones sticking out."

I walked to the ditch. Some of the black people were sitting on the ditch bank, beyond the ditch, hunkering in a squat. Every time the blue light of the police car rotated, the white eyes in the black people shone from the ditch bank. The black people were sitting still, looking in the ditch. The ditch was wide near the culvert where the creek ran under the road and the shoulder was narrow. Cars were coming by, slowing down, and people were looking around from inside the cars, looking at the wrecked station wagon and the black people on the ditch bank. The cars came by slow and dimmed their lights, and when they saw Sammy in the ditch they slowed to a crawl. Sammy was in the ditch on his side with his four feet sticking straight out and stiff. His eyes were open and only the white showed. He was bloated, relaxed, the bulk of his body pushed up through his frame, and on top of his frame was a pool of blood.

"That yo' bull?"

"Yes, sir," I said to the black people on the bank.

It was a woman. She had on a man's suit and hat and white shirt and she was fat so her clothes were tight, brown or grey and stained.

"How th' hell I s'posed to get to work?" She talked like a man. "Whut th' hell I s'posed to do? Walk?"

"I think my insurance will do it."

"Do whut? Yo' 'surance gonna take me to work?"

"The patrolman will tell you what to do. I'm sorry about the car. I'm glad you're not hurt. I've got to go."

"That yo' cow?" She was the only one who spoke. "Can't you keep yo' cow from gettin' out no fence? Come on—give us a ride home, mista."

"I'm sorry but I've got to go."

"Come on, mista!" she shouted.

I walked away, past Sammy, down the shoulder to James Louis. The patrolman was writing on a pad.

"Y'all go on," he said. "Don't worry about the niggers." He said he'd get somebody to haul Sammy out to our farm to get him off the side of the road.

Back on the pavement I drove fast with my flashers on. We counted and Judy breathed like we had practiced every night for months.

"What are you counting?" I asked, checking to make sure the flashers were on. I accelerated out of the curves and drove with both hands, feeling the car on the road, taking the power James Louis had.

"New Oldsmobiles." She giggled as she exhaled. "Thirty-seven is green and brown, thirty-eight is blue and white, thirty-nine is grey and black."

As she inhaled I said, "When they teach that course they ought to have one class in a car so we'd know how to do it in a car."

She exhaled. "Don't make me laugh. Forty is two-tone tan, forty-one is yellow and white . . ."

We came to the highway. I slowed for the stop sign and saw that nobody was coming; then, starting in a slow roll in second, I wound James Louis in each gear. The four barrels cut in when the timing advanced and the mufflers sounded at the high RPM.

Judy rubbed below her belly. "I'm still dripping water." The seat was wet, and she wiped the water with the tissues she had brought in case she cried. "Sammy was a great bull. I wonder why he busted out to follow that cow."

"She was in heat."

"He shouldn't have been able to bust out. Oh, God! Oh, Truck, something's happening. Oh, shit!"

"Start counting." I was watching the road, checking the gauges, watching the side roads, moving my eyes to catch motion. "Count seedless grapes. Remember? One seedless grape, two seedless grapes . . . Come on."

"Why did you have to stop?" She was screaming. "You knew I was ready and you stopped for that fucking bull." She was holding her belly with both hands. Her shoulders were forward and tense and she turned her head up and cried, "Oh, shit!" She cried, "Oh, no!"

"Two seedless grapes. Come on—real slow. Three seedless grapes. *Do it,* damn it!"

Her arm sprang toward me but she missed and clutched the steering wheel instead and held it as she screamed. I rammed my knee into the back of the steering wheel to hold it firm. I hit her left cheek with the back of my closed right fist. She let go of the wheel. I threw her to the other side of the seat. We ran off the pavement onto the shoulder and I slowed the car in the rutty grass. I pinned Judy against the door with my forearm. The bouncing made her hold the seat and door with both hands. She whimpered. I steered onto the pavement.

Judy didn't scream anymore on the way to the hospital. I helped her count and she tried to breathe, but she couldn't get the rhythm. She sat there grunting. We went to the emergency entrance and got her to the doctors, and by the time I parked and found her they had given her a painkiller.

What happened after that was what I had expected—we had seen all the films of births and hospital procedures and the location of all the facilities—except that the baby was a girl, not a boy like I had expected.

Judy was hurting, in and out of a drowsy sleep, while they cleaned and tested the baby. I called Momma and Daddy and told them it was a girl, and we had named her Wendy. By then it was late morning. I noticed I smelled bad and was tired. The doctor told me to go home and clean up and get some rest and come back later because Judy and the baby both needed to rest and they would both be glad to see me later. He told me to come back about dark.

I parked James Louis in front of the house and shut him down. I figured it was about noon, a bright day. Sammy was lying in the garden on his side. It was warm in the sun. I guessed the policeman had called Mister Alcie and told him what had happened because all the policemen knew Mister Alcie, and I figured Mister Alcie had hauled Sammy from the road ditch to my garden. Mister Alcie was the only person who knew I would bury my dead animals under the garden. I did not want to go into the house. All I could think to do was cry. I didn't want to see Sammy up close yet. I went toward the pasture. I didn't bother to wipe the snot and tears that ran over my mouth. The cows saw me and lowed. They were in the bottom near the pond, and, thinking I might want to feed them some apples, they came up the hill to the fence. I was at the fence waiting for them. It took a long time for them to come up the big green hill, and when they got there they looked at me funny because they had never seen me cry or heard me sobbing. I had to laugh while I was crying because they looked at me so funny.

All the cows had steel chains around their necks with numbers stamped in oval brass tags that hung from the chains. The chains and tags rattled together when the cows moved. When the rattling stopped I stopped crying. They were all standing still looking at me. Sammy's Momma too.

"Hey, Sammy's Momma," I said. "You seen Sammy over there?"

Some of the cows lowed.

"I got a baby girl."

Sammy's Momma was doing just like the other cows.

"You look good," I told her. "You look better than I thought you'd ever look." I wiped the snot and tears on my forearm. "Remember the night Sammy was born? That was some night. That vet came out. Judy got pissed off because she thought you were dead. And Sammy was born. He sure did grow up pretty."

The cows started to wander and look around and nibble at the grass, sticking their tongues out as their heads swung past the grass, circling the grass with their tongues, ripping at the clumps of grass, looking up before going for more, and all the time walking away, their chains rattling.

I went to the garden and spent the rest of the daylight digging a hole big enough to bury Sammy, deep enough to pack three feet of dirt over his carcass.

HEPZEBIAH
NOVEMBER 10, 1981

Driving James Louis in the meadow at noon is what I do every day, although it's not really a meadow and I stopped enjoying it when Beth came one time and told me people were saying I was crazy. It's really a grassy hillside that was terraced by government workers a long time ago because the topsoil had been washed into the creek bottom, because people had raised cotton on the same land, year after year, and the land could not support it, and all the topsoil that did not wash to the bottom leached.

The terraces are on the contour, and from the porch of my place on the hill, in the edge of the woods, I look across the terraced, grassy field at the creek, at the dirt road that comes perpendicular to the bottom, and, through the trees so it is barely visible in winter and invisible in summer when the broadleaves flower, at Buck Winston's shack near the store. It is really mine. I bought it from Mister Alcie Pace. I paid for it with the money I earned in the war. I let Buck Winston stay and run the store because he's Earl's daddy, and I always will because I want Earl to owe me one, always, and he will because that chickenshit fucker stayed home. The Hainted Place is mine, the meadow and the creek bottom and woods and the shack and store where Buck Winston stays. All I can see. It's mine. Buck Winston's shack has never been painted, and when I see it from my porch, through the trees in winter, it looks like the trees.

When I'm driving James Louis in the meadow at noon I can see the whole weathered shack: tin roof; old, grown-up shrubs; dirt yard; big oaks; rutted driveway. It sits on stone piers and has moved through the years so it leans, sometimes between the piers and sometimes on an edge, and the leanings and vertical and horizontal timbers are what give it the same basic lines as the trees when I am on the porch in winter. I have to drive James Louis up the hill on the dirt road to see the store. I can't see it at all from down here.

Uncle Goody shot a boy scout and killed him dead when he lived here. It was when I was little, before he moved to the sexton's house behind the church. I know he went to jail, but I don't think it was for shooting the boy scout. I think it was for something else. Now I live in the old Hainted Place, me and Bean and the cats. It's nice because I always stay dry and nobody bothers us. Some of them used to come but not anymore. I sit on the porch and wait until noon so I can drive James Louis. Nobody comes but Beth, and she brings food.

I've been up for an hour, cooked breakfast and smoked a joint. The rocker squeaks as it moves in a slow, steady motion. The music on the easy-listening station sounds like leaves falling, strings and oboes, muted trumpets. My full, untrimmed beard hangs like a shadow from my chin and face. Sometimes I feel it and sometimes I don't. I usually don't feel it when I'm stoned, like I don't feel the air or my last pair of jungle skivvies, which is all I wear. I'm a part of it all. We're all just one big thing, and that's good, so I stay stoned. My hair rests on my shoulders, curled at the ends, flowing from underneath my hat. I've been developing the wrinkles on my brow and at the corners of my eyes, and my cheeks hold half-moon-shaped lines like crevasses welded into my face. If somebody is watching from the woods I want them to think that I am thinking instead of just sitting on my ass, so I look like I'm

thinking and wrinkle my face and hope the wrinkles get permanent so I can have a function.

A big truck slows on the dirt road and turns up the driveway
toward my shack, the low gear grinding unevenly, the busted
muffler amplifying the noise of the engine. Bean starts barking
and wagging his tail, although I've told him not to wag his tail
while he barks because of the conflicting signals. The vehicle is
in front of the shack, motionless, engine quiet. The driver, old,
wrinkled, a grey stubble of beard, a cigarette in his mouth, looks
at Bean and around the yard.

"Need somebody t' pick up yer garbage?"

"Sure don't."

"Somebody else already picking it up?"

"I ain't got any."

The driver stares at me in my skivvies, then cranks his monster
and leaves with Bean barking, noise and smoke everywhere. I go
into the shack which is cluttered with the food wrappers and cans
and dishes and clothes from two weeks of my existence. The cats
are coming in, one at a time, sniffing and scratching the leftover
scraps of food, darting after bugs, and crouching low against the
walls. It smells old. This place is all old, all wood—small boards on
the walls and ceiling, big boards on the floor. They have given me
some furniture that's old and a used radio. The radio stays on all
the time.

I sing aloud. I know all the words. Sometimes I mouth them,
like I'm singing. Sometimes I sit and absorb the music and the
story of the song without making any noise. Sometimes I push it
further in, blank it out, use it as a backdrop, a setting for the
thoughts that come and stay and accumulate and never leave; and
when I sing aloud at night I scream. The screaming scares Bean
and makes him howl.

It must be almost ten, so I'd better watch. There's a break in the
trees, not across the meadow and the terraces but right through
the trees. Through the window I can see the road and catch a
glimpse of anything that is coming down the hill toward the

creek. I can also look in the bottom, below the meadow, and see anything that crosses Cocaine Bridge and goes uphill away from the creek. The mail comes about ten unless the mail lady is late.

I hum quietly, looking for shoes and shorts, putting them on as I find them, then go through the open door and whistle up Bean, who comes from the woods and his daily routine of pissing on trees and following sunspots as they snake their way through our place. The mail lady crosses Cocaine Bridge and slows and stops at my mailbox. She hesitates, then dashes off. I look through the break in the trees and there he is, Buck Winston walking.

Buck Winston walks at exactly ten every day. He has a clock at the store, and when the second hand hits ten he leaves the store open and always takes the same number of steps between the store and the creek, and he always walks hard in the dirt on the road because when he gets to the creek and turns around to go back to the store he walks in the same footsteps he walked in coming down the hill, and he always carries his stopwatch so he can make sure it takes him the same number of seconds to walk the same number of steps from the store to the creek and back. He does it every day. If I know the mail has come and I catch a glimpse of Buck Winston walking, through the break in the trees, I go down the driveway to the mailbox so I can look at Buck and say, "Hello, Mister Winston. Out walking, huh?" and he mashes the stem on his stopwatch and freezes in his steps, so he doesn't mess up his system, and says, "Hello, Truck. How's the weather?"

My jogging shoes are worn on the bottom, paper thin, but the tops and sides are strong enough to protect me from sticks and briars when I walk through the meadow or the woods, and I keep the driveway free of rocks, smooth with only dirt. If I see or feel a small rock I always stop and chunk it aside so I don't have to get any new jogging shoes. Bean ranges to the sides of the driveway, sniffing for mice or litter. A hawk circles high, screeching and looking for exposed prey in the dying weeds. One of the cats makes a high-speed pass in front of Bean, challenging, and Bean practices his sharp turns and bark control while running. The cat finds a sweet gum tree and rests on the lowest limb hissing. Bean gets maximum height out of a two-legged jump, then forgets the cat and catches up with me as I get near the mailbox. He's breathing hard.

I look in the mailbox. There's a handout, one of these things everybody gets one of; then I look up at Buck, who is right there.

"Hello, Mister Winston. Out walking, huh?"

He's got a grey crew cut and a walking stick and a liquor face, little red lines, and a big belly and suspenders. He mashes the stem on his stopwatch and freezes in his steps and says, "Hello, Truck. How's the weather?"

"Won't be long before rain sets in. Had three freezes."

"You got any small plastic bags?"

"No, sir."

He walks toward me, hitting the stopwatch and measuring his steps and hitting it again, thinking for a moment. He reaches into the hip pocket of his serge britches and pulls out a handful of small plastic bags. He peels one off and gives it to me. "Keep this. You need it in case you find some ripe berries or a small chicken."

I take the bag. "Thank you. You got any nail clippers at the store?"

"Nail clippers?"

"Nail clippers. You know—you twist the little thing around and you can clip your nails and it's got an emery board so you can file your nails?"

"Nail clippers. I got some at the store."

"Reckon you could bring me some tomorrow when ya take your walk?"

"Well, I got 'em at the store."

"I need nail clippers so I can clip my nails. See my nails?" I hold my hands up palms-down so he can see my claws. "They're gettin' to where they hurt me when I scratch."

"I got some at the store."

"I'm real busy. I can't come to the store. I was thinking maybe you could bring me some tomorrow when you take your walk."

"People come to the store and buy stuff."

"This is like a whole new idea. You bring me some nail clippers tomorrow, down here, and I'll give you something that's worth as much as the nail clippers."

He grins like a child. "What is it?"

"Well, I don't know yet. But I'll bring something down here that's worth as much as the clippers."

The idea seems to suit him, and he punches the stem on his stopwatch and walks toward the creek, pacing evenly, lunging with each step.

I go up the driveway, slowly, reading the handout about a place where you can buy some land near a lake and get away from everything and ride boats and swim and laugh. At the shack I throw the handout on the floor of the porch and sit in the rocker and smoke another joint, green stuff because it's not noon yet. I smoke the green stuff that I grow myself in the mornings. After driving James Louis in the meadow at noon I switch to the brown stuff I buy from a cop in Piedmont. At night when I get James Louis gassed up and loaded I smoke the red stuff I get when me and Son make a run.

Beth's coming up the driveway in her little car that was built in one of the countries that lost the war. Sometimes she blows the horn to let me know. Today she drives right into the yard and stops. She gets out. She must have the day off, but she's in work clothes, skirt and blouse. She's pretty. Looks like me except no beard. I laugh. She looks at my eyes. She knows I've smoked.

"Want to ride with me to town?"

"What's today?"

"Tuesday. I went by the parsonage and saw Momma and Daddy. Let's go to town. I need to pick up a few things. Then we can have lunch and I'll bring you back out here." She leans on a porch post and folds her arms in front of her.

"I'd better not," I say. "I'm working some at night. I need rest."

She goes into the shack and picks up clothes that are scattered on the floor and the dresser and the bed. She smells each piece of clothing and puts the ones that smell bad in one pile and the ones that can be worn again in a different pile.

"I can do that later," I say. I'm on the porch rocking.

"Let somebody help you." She keeps picking up.

"Uncle Goody helps me."

It's a grey day. The trees are almost naked and stand like disfigured giants. Beth fiddles for a while, then comes to the porch. "Have you seen Wendy?"

"No. But Earl wrote me a letter. Said last month's check didn't clear the bank. Said if I don't have a cashier's check in his office by next Monday I'll have trouble." I yawn, clear my throat and cough. "So I walked up to the store and called the asshole. Told him to run my check back through, that it's good now. He says, 'I don't know that to be true.' So I told him he don't know what trouble is. He's gonna hide behind the skirts of some bad laws and cause me trouble? He sends me shit in the mail telling me I'm gonna have trouble? I told him trouble is when his nose gets moved over beside his ear so his own crazy daddy don't recognize him, and that's gonna happen to him if he sends me any more shit in the mail saying I'm gonna have trouble. He says, 'Some of us are civilized, and we have laws that make us that way. There's a little girl and a nice lady who are suffering because you abandoned them and refuse to support them.' And I asked him if civilized people refuse to fight for their country, and he hung up."

Beth is standing, watching. "Is Judy working?"

"I don't know what she's doing, except she talks to Earl every day, tells him all the trash she can think of about me, and he's taking care of her with the judges and getting court orders telling me to do things they know I can't do. Wendy is her only weapon. She uses my baby and that asshole Earl. All he used to talk about was getting off the Hainted Place. Now he's gonna steal half of it from me, and he hasn't done a thing to earn it."

"Don't you think—"

"He's working for them."

"Who are 'they'?"

"I don't know, but there's a 'they' somewhere, and they must think I know too much, and it's Earl's job to knock me on my ass and keep me there." I take a cigarette from a pack near the porch post and light it.

"Momma and Daddy don't know what to do. They asked me if I'd try to find out what you need, what you want to do."

"I'd be content to fuck and fight. Other animals do that—lions and some birds—and I was good at it."

"That was just for a while, Truck."

"When they came to see Momma and Daddy and told them I was missing? You think that was just a while?"

"All the time you were there I wondered what you were doing, especially when you were missing. Then when we found out you were okay—"

"You think I was okay?" I am shouting. "Do I look like I'm okay? All that time they said I was missing I wasn't missing. I was *there!*"

She leans over and kisses me on the cheek, then goes to her car and comes back with a full grocery bag and goes into the shack. "Sure you don't want to go to town?" She comes out with a pile of dirty clothes under one arm.

"I need to do some stuff around here."

"Please go see Momma and Daddy. They miss you."

She goes down the steps. I wait until she gets in her car and as she starts the car and moves toward the driveway I find a joint. It's not dark yet. It's not even noon. But I find some of the red stuff and I smoke it.

Momma has on an old housecoat that she made. Her hair is pure white and her skin is smooth and clear in spite of her age. The kitchen smells like fresh-baked bread and mustard greens, the leftovers from supper and tomorrow's lunch, which are pushed to one side of the table to make room for our game. Daddy is whistling hymns in his study while he works on his sermon. The white plastic radio beside the sink is playing soft church music. The Christmas tablecloth is on the table.

"You must have the 'Q,' " I say.

Momma looks up through the top part of her bifocals, then shifts her view back through the thick part at the bottom of her glasses to her letters on the little wooden letter holder.

"How do you know?"

"You always put it at one end by itself, like you don't want to have to deal with it or something."

Momma smiles, puts five letters on the Scrabble board and says, "'Quasar,' Q-U-A-S-A-R. Forty-five points."

"Sorry I brought it up."

She removes her glasses and puts them on the table and smiles at me. "I'm glad you came, Truck. Your turn."

"I've been busy."

I study my letters. I glance back and forth between the board and my letters. "'Hate.'" I put the letters on the board and straighten them one at the time. "Eight."

Momma asks, "When will we get to see Wendy again?"

"I'm supposed to see her next month."

"I had hoped Judy would come by and visit."

"It's your turn."

Momma studies her letters and the board. She folds her hands in her lap. "I had a beau once," she says, "when I was in seminary. There was no money then, so all the students had to work to keep the school going. I cooked breakfast every morning, starting with a big pot of grits at four o'clock. I baked all the pies, cakes, bread, and corn bread for the noon and evening meals. After a two-hour break I went to class all afternoon.

"My friend went to class in the mornings. He worked on the farm in the afternoons and did the evening milking. We met every day for lunch beside a pond, a picnic in the pasture by the lunch room, and studied together and talked—every day except Sunday. We went to church on Sunday. The man who ran the farm had a white German shepherd that came out every day and sat with us. We gave the dog our leftover food." She smiles and leans toward me, onto the table, over the game we are playing. "My friend graduated and I had another year. He went off to seminary. We were planning for both of us to finish school, then decide if it would be right to marry. Six weeks after he left I got a letter saying he had met someone and he appreciated my friendship." She looks at her letters and moves them around on her holder. "I thought I wouldn't live, that there was no reason to keep existing. The dog seemed to understand when I told him about it every day. On Sunday, when I didn't take a break down by the pond but went back to my room to get ready for church, I could look out the window of my room and see the white shepherd waiting for me in the pasture by the water."

"How long did it take you to get over it?"

"Six or seven months, I guess. Then I met your father." She puts some letters on the board. "Twelve." She writes the figure on a pad and adds the score. "Judy is humiliated and hurt and scared, Horace."

"I am too, Momma."

"What went wrong?"

"Momma . . ."

"Don't fight her. The Lord says all vengeance belongs to him. And don't judge her. It'll be Wendy who suffers in a fight."

"Do I just sit still, let her and Earl take my land?"

" 'May the words of my mouth and the meditations of my heart be acceptable in thy sight, O Lord, my strength and my redeemer.' "

I go to the pantry and open a jar of candy mints. There have always been mints in the pantry. I pop two in my mouth. I go to the sink and draw a glass of water and drink the water. I return to the table.

Daddy comes into the kitchen. "Who wants popcorn?" He goes to the pantry and starts looking through the pots and pans and appliances.

Momma says, "That sounds good."

"How about you, Horace?"

"Okay."

"Where's that pot I like to cook popcorn in?"

Momma says, "Look in the cabinet beside the refrigerator," then to me, "Whose turn is it?"

"Mine."

Daddy keeps looking in the cabinet and says, "Earl ought to be horse-whipped."

"I guess Earl's doing the best he can," I say.

HEPZEBIAH
NOVEMBER 11, 1981

The kerosene lamp on the table beside the board flickers from the movement of the air, throwing splotches of light and shadows. The room holds the musty smell of lamp fumes, grease, and smoke from old pine wood.

Uncle Goody never studies his moves. The pace he sets makes me go fast, and I'm always reacting to him instead of acting. I know all these things, but he always stays ahead. "It's in my blood," he says. That's how he explains it.

"You're never consistent," I say. "I sit here and figure why you win. Then you start different and I don't know what you're doing."

"I jus' moves the men. The Lawd 'cides where they go." Then he jumps one of my checkers and says, "Mek me a king, boy."

We play checkers until Son makes a noise and moves in his bed. I stand and get my coat off a nail. The door is made of sheeting with back braces on a diagonal, like the doors on barns. As I leave, Uncle Goody tells me Son will be ready by the time I get my load.

I check the oil and the water in James Louis. I crank him and let him idle, and I check the tires and the bolts that hold the shocks. When I first start out I keep a low RPM and adjust the mirrors and listen to the engine, rolling along slow in high gear;

then when the engine sounds right and I come to a straightaway, I check everything at high RPM. I like to smoke some of the red stuff before I go by myself to get my load.

James Louis's paint has faded. The muffler and front fender are loose. I turn off Snakey Road onto the half-mile-long dirt path that goes between Mister Alcie's tobacco barns. The car rattles. I drive slow. The building at the end of the path is rectangular and made of concrete block painted white and has no windows. The roof is flat and tarred. On the front, facing the path, is a sectioned garage door that can be raised and slid under the flat ceiling. A security light is on a pole. Cars are parked beside some shrubs and bushes. On one of the cars two cats are lying on their bellies. Mister Alcie's dog, Erastus, barks, then wanders toward James Louis as we stop and go silent and I get out.

"Hello, 'Rastus."

He wags his tail and smells Bean's scent on me. I look around the area lit by the security light and inside all the cars. There are voices inside the building. It is a clear night, cool but not chilly yet. A man appears at a corner of the building. He looks like a Yankee. Erastus sits and watches me.

"Come in." The man walks back into the shadows.

"I'll wait out here," I say.

He leaves. I go to the car and lean on it. Erastus follows me.

"They got a password?" I smile at the dog. "What is it?"

A different man appears. "Can I hep ya?" He is a farmer in heavy clothes and a baseball cap.

"Here to see Mister Alcie."

He looks at James Louis, then leads me behind the building. I follow him through a door, from the dark of night to a room lit by bare bulbs and warm from a big log burner in the corner. Some men are playing poker on a green felt table by the fire. There are two late-model cars in the shadows near the front of the room, with their engines and transmissions out and torn apart. Tools and machines are scattered with dirty rags on them.

The floor is covered with a thick layer of hardened grease and sawdust and oil and tobacco juice. Two pretty young girls are sitting on an old school-bus seat drinking whiskey out of glasses. They are wearing dresses. Mister Alcie is at a work table cleaning an intake manifold and whistling. Another man is in a straight chair at a desk working with papers. Mister Alcie looks up when we walk toward him. He's dressed like a farmer.

"You want me to come over here tonight?" I ask.

"Need you to make a run."

I follow him out the back door. Some of the people in the room look and nod. It is quiet in the room. We go outside to the clear night and walk down a dirt path until we come to a three-story barn that was never painted and has weathered grey. There is a two-ton flatbed inside with a tarp over it. Some calves are in a stall and two horses are standing at the other open end of the barn. The animals watch us from the shadows. Mister Alcie lifts the edge of the tarp.

"Take ten bundles," he says. "Everybody's bought except Swanson County. Deliver nine and you keep one. This is some good marijuana. We grew it here on the place. Pure ripe buds. Female stuff. Ten-pound bundles." He tells me where to deliver the bundles.

It was the spring of 1980 when we started making these runs. It took several tries to figure the best way to handle Son. We finally built some rails out of old lumber. We run his wheelchair off the porch onto the rails and slide him into the passenger seat in James Louis. I buckle him in and lean his head on the back of the seat so he can see. Uncle Goody waves from the porch as we leave.

The weight in the trunk makes James Louis hug the road. There is a layer of clouds up high and no fog. We work our way on the country roads to the four-lane highway, gearing up for the fast lane. Son rocks twice, then sits still. His head is tilted on the back of the seat so he sees everything sideways. The towels around his neck are pinned tight. He doesn't drool much when he's happy. I set my speed. The gauges look good.

we?" I put the lights on bright and hug the white line. James Louis is humming on the road. Son rolls his head straight up, then back sideways. "Did I tell you about the night in Okinawa when me and Pete went to the Air Force 'O' club and everybody got sauced and we started playing carrier landings with the Air Force turds, and I got the crotch of my flight suit caught on the edge of the table and Pete went running into the dining room and screamed, 'Truck got his dick caught on a table!' and the base commander's wife fainted? I know I told you about the time we went into Olongopo to get a hand job and when the women started beating our dicks we noticed they had big calluses on their hands from chopping rice all day with homemade hoes, and we paid them their money but didn't let 'em beat our dicks anymore. Remember me telling you about that? We went back out to the base and raced go-carts. That was the longest night of my life.

"You say, 'The longest night?' and I have to say, 'No, not the longest night.' You want to know what was the longest night? Mess Night."

Son never moves when I'm talking to him in James Louis. James Louis is tight on the highway. It has gotten chilly and I keep the windows down and the heater on. Son's straps are tight. He is still. I spit out the window at the end of every curve.

"So you say, 'Mess Night? I never heard about Mess Night.' Well, let me tell you." The tachometer is stable. "It was the night our training was over and we got our orders. The idea was to put on fancy uniforms and go to this formal meal with a bunch of high-ranking officers and get real drunk without losing your couth. You stand around for an hour drinking whiskey, chatting with the generals and colonels. Then the drum-and-bugle corps marches through, and you follow them into the dining room like the Pied Piper. There were a hundred of us lieutenants, and the dining room had these long tables running parallel to each other with a head table at one end, and all the tables were covered with linen, crystal wine glasses, china plates and bowls, sterling silver. They had three forks and several knives and spoons. They had

place cards at every seat, and me and Pete wandered around and
found our places. We were side by side because of the alphabet.
Then the adjutant introduced the heavies and they marched in
according to their rank. The colonels were first, then the generals,
then General Windsor, the commander of Her Majesty's Royal
Marines, and the drums and bugles were still playing."

Son is not moving and he's not drooling. *Engine is a hundred
and eighty degrees, Son. Three thousand RPM. Oil pressure good.
No lights.* We leave the four-lane for a two-lane country road that
is hilly. We are in the flatlands. The road is straight. There are
some hills but no traffic.

"Well, we all sat down to eat, lieutenants at the long tables and
the heavies at the head table. They had these big, funny-looking
bottles of wine on the tables. Carafes. They brought out another
kind of wine in a regular bottle and some fish didn't have a crust
on it. The waiters were the enlisted men who had been the
drummers and the buglers, and they were all running around.
They brought vegetables and beef, more wine, different kinds of
wine, red, pink, white—all the wine you could drink. We used all
the different plates and looked around to see which forks we were
supposed to use.

"Like I said, Pete was next to me. I'd seen Pete drunk before,
lots of times, but that night he was good and drunk. He couldn't
quit grinning. I knew he was getting ready to bet on something.
He leaned over to me when the waiters were picking up the dishes
and said, 'I bet there's not any wine left in this room when this
cluster fuck is over,' and I bet him a fifth of Jack Daniel's there
would be some somewhere."

I adjust Son's towels, and I wipe his face. He is slobbering some,
but he is still.

"The only things left on the tables were carafes and glasses and
some dishes with food on them that people hadn't finished. The
heavies started talking, colonels first, then generals. They talked
about the rigorous training and the preparation we had just
finished, and the fact that we were better prepared than they were

when they were lieutenants. Then they introduced the commander of Her Majesty's Royal Marines. We all stood up to clap
when he walked to the middle of the head table and did a left face
toward us. Pete was reconnoitering our table, looking for carafes
or glasses with wine in them. When everybody else finished
clapping and sat down, Pete stayed standing till he spotted a carafe
near the front with some wine in it, then he sat down. General
Windsor started a speech about esprit de corps and how one man
who believes in something can get together with a bunch of other
men who believe in the same thing, and if they're all serious and
willing to work and don't mind spending a little time, there is no
limit to what they can do. Pete was sitting there bleary-eyed,
nodding his head. He put his elbows on the table and eased himself
up onto the table. He started crawling down the table toward that
carafe with the wine in it. He tried to move the empty carafes and
glasses out of the way as he crawled along, but every now and then
he'd knock something over. The lieutenants facing the front
turned to him as he crawled by. They sat back in their chairs
making way for him to pass, then looked back at General Windsor,
who was talking about courage. He was talking about what it's like
the first time in war and how the people around you are scared
too—about death and honor, stuff like that. General Windsor saw
Pete crawling down the table but he kept right on making his
speech.

"Pete got to the carafe up near the front. He picked it up and
looked at the wine in it and stood on his knees on the table. It was
red wine. He turned that carafe up and took a big slug of it. General
Windsor stopped talking. Pete puked a purple projectile ten feet
down the table straight toward a colonel. Then he wiped his mouth
with the back of his hand and turned that carafe up and chugged
all the wine and swallowed it and looked around the room to make
sure there wasn't any more wine anywhere. Everybody was
looking at him. He was stinking, sitting in the puke on his knees.
When Pete saw there wasn't any more wine, he passed out on the

table. And General Windsor said, 'Gentlemen, I give you a great marine!' And we all cheered and sat down and left Pete lying there on the table passed out in his puke."

We are close to Swanson County. The only sounds are the engine humming and the tires on the pavement and the wind. When I lean out to spit, the cold wind hits my face, makes me alert. I watch everything that moves beside the road, what the machine is doing, and the rearview mirror, and try to see on the other side of each hill. Son is happy and still.

"General Windsor changed his speech and told us how war is a whore and a man's got to have her. He said if a male of the species didn't go to war then that creature never became a man. That was the night everybody got their orders. Pete won the bet. There wasn't any wine left. Me and Pete both got orders to Vietnam. That's what we wanted."

We cross the Swanson County line. The land is flat and the roads are wider and mostly straight and level. Headlights come on bright a few feet behind us and a blue light flashes and a siren sounds. I slam on the brakes. The car behind drops back, then accelerates to pass. Son moves both hands and rolls his head.

"Deputy sheriff," I tell Son. "That's what it says on that car."

I stop and the car passes and stops in front of us. Two men get out. I sit tight. They leave their lights on. They have on brown outfits with brown belts. Their pocket covers, hats, and ties are black. Their badges are shiny metal. One man comes to each side of James Louis. Son's head is toward me. He is trying to focus.

The man on my side shines his light into my eyes. "Out kinda late, ain't ya?" he says.

"Yes, sir," I say.

He shines his light toward Son. The other man has backed away and is shining his light on James Louis—the tires, the trunk, underneath.

"Who's your friend there?"

I call, "Son!"

Son rolls his head and says, "Auunnnuugh."

"Goddamn!" He shines his flashlight into Son's face. "Look at this nigger, Charles!"

The other man quits looking at James Louis, shines his light into Son's face.

"Goddamn! What you got this nigger on?"

"Look at that shit comin' outa that nigger's mouth!"

"What's wrong with this nigger, Buddy?" They look at me with the lights.

"He's been taken," I say.

They look back at Son. He's rolling his head, trying to focus.

"Get this nigger outa here. What you doin' ridin' around with a nigger like this?"

"He's my friend."

"Goddamn! You get outa here. Don't you come back around here with this nigger."

Uncle Goody jumps a red one and says, "Mek me a king, boy."

I put a black player atop another black one on the edge of the board closest to me. "Ever play for money?"

"Won't no money. Played fo' three days onest, long time ago. We ain't stop fo' three days." He moves one of his men. "I'z still a youngun, hepin' Daddy cure 'bacca. We'z stayin' up all night tendin' the fires in the barns an' choppin' wood. M'ol' daddy, he cured the best 'bacca in these parts, an' he didn' take no chances on it not doin' right. If'n we won't choppin' or tendin', we wuz playin' checkies, fo' three days."

I jump one of his men and take it off the board and watch for him to react.

"We got stopped tonight," I say.

Uncle Goody says, "I know'd it when ya brung Son in."

We sit quietly without making a move.

"What did you go to jail for?"

"Fo' years an' fo' days I spent in the fed'ral pen. Didn't do nothin' fo' fo' years an' fo' days. Dat wuz for I'z growed good. I'z drivin' a wagonload o' whiskey to d' city an' wuz all dem ol' hosses could do to pull it. Men in a car, dey pulls up 'side me and tells me to get off'n the road, tells me I ain't s'posed to be totin' all dat whiskey. Dey puts me in the pen." He looks at the board. "Ya been watchin' ol' Goody play, ain't ya, boy?"

I smile and keep my head down, toward the board.

"Mista Alcie, he done bought off all the local laws, couldn't do nothin' w'dem fed'ral laws. I jus' pulled my time."

"You reckon it was worth it?"

"I figured it wuz." He studies the board and moves one of his players, and his move surprises me. He finishes winning. He goes to check on Son and I set the board. It is quiet except for Son's moans.

HEPZEBIAH
DECEMBER 1981

Beth told me I had to get some work. She told me she would not bring any more food until I got a job. I told her I had to work at night. She said if I had to work at night newspapers was the best job around. I told her newspapers are written by leftist cock-suckers. And I told her I did not want to go get my own food because when I went to the store people looked at me funny. Beth told me who to call at the newspaper in the city to get the job. I called them. Now when I run the newspapers at night I don't see anybody unless I want to, and nobody sees me unless I want them to. But running every night is too much for Son, so he stays at home, except when we run for Mister Alcie.

This morning I was alone on the dark, two-lane road. I slowed James Louis before turning into the lighted, gravelly parking lot. Tires plopped into mud holes and James Louis waddled on his chassis past the line of Whites and Freightliners and Macks that were still and dark in a neat row with their big diesel engines running and their drivers asleep inside. I pulled into the streak of light that shone from the restaurant through the rain and I parked.

The building was made of concrete blocks and had a flat roof. Some of the small neon tubes that lined the outside of the overhang were lit, some flashed intermittently, and some were dark. A concrete island with gas pumps sticking up in the middle of the parking lot had its own lights, and to the north of the building was a lighted shelter where the truckers could change tires and work on their engines. Once the car was stopped I got out and reached back in through the open window and pushed in the knob that turned the lights off but left the motor and windshield wipers running. Then I ran from the car to the entranceway, braced against the rain, and pushed the glass door so it swung open into the room where the upbeat country song was playing. I stomped my feet in my old flight boots and brushed some water off my flight jacket and jeans.

The woman behind the counter stopped her work and smiled. She was fat, especially above her elbows on the back of her arms, and had jet-black teased hair, heavy makeup, and a white waitress outfit. She moved from the half-cleaned grill to the coffee machine and took a Styrofoam cup from the top of a pile of cups and poured it full of coffee with cream and sugar. She put a straw through the hole in a plastic lid and put the lid on the cup.

"The rain's nasty," I said.

The woman smiled and said, "This is one of them nights when I'm glad I work in here instead of out there." She motioned toward the front wall where big sheets of glass reflected an image of us standing near the counter in the lighted room. She put the cup of coffee on the counter in front of me.

The sound of air rushing through a tight space made me turn toward the front where a man swung the glass door open. He walked into the room brushing off his coat. He had on a pea coat, a sock cap, jeans, and jungle boots. He was small. He looked like a Yankee. He approached the counter and sat on a stool.

I turned to the woman. "Lemme have some square nabs."

She reached into the glass case beneath the cash register and pulled out a pack of nabs and put it on the counter. "Thirty-four."

I put a handful of change beside it and started counting.

The man was on the second stool down from me. "Which way

you headed?" he asked. His hair stuck out from under the sock cap in places. He had a thick beard and was pale, his face was puffed. His eyes were swollen, moist and red.

"North."

"As far as the next truck stop?"

"Yeah. That help you any?"

"Beats walking."

I recounted the change on the counter, picked up the coffee and nabs, and started toward the front and the door. The man slipped off the stool. I changed the cup of coffee from one hand to the other and used the free hand to open the door, allowing the man to move past. I followed him into the rain and pulled the zipper on my jacket up until I had to tilt my head back to keep the zipper out of my beard; then I pulled the zipper up as far as it would go under my chin, next to the small, thin hairs of my beard that grow in the folds of skin.

The man looked into my eyes. "You in 'Nam?" he asked, then he looked toward the gas pumps and the parking lot and trucks in the rain.

"Yeah. Were you?"

"Yeah."

Outside the range of the lights it was dark. There were no lights at houses, and there was no traffic. The people who used the old farm-to-market road were loading yesterday's produce on their pickups and two-ton flatbeds. It would be five o'clock, just before dawn, when they started driving the old road to the city and stopped at the truck stop for coffee and news.

We stepped backward, up against the building, under the overhang, out of the rain, behind a thick sheet of water that dripped off the flat roof.

"Where are you headed?"

"Philadelphia." The man reached into his trousers pocket. He smiled and shifted from one foot to the other and moved his gaze from my face to the parked trucks to some puddles. "You out at night in 'Nam?"

"Yeah."

"I was on night patrol," he said. "They sent us into Laos and they were gonna pick us up, you know?"

I said, "Yeah."

He said, "I was out there fourteen weeks. Somebody just *happened* to spot me one day . . . from th' air? You know? They just *happened* to see me? And they said they'd been looking for me but thought I was dead." He reached into his field-jacket pocket. "All that time?" He fumbled around, then pulled out a cigarette and some matches. "You smoke?"

I shook my head.

"I got to where I liked them woods at night. Couldn't nobody see me, you know?" He was staring at the rain and the dark.

"Yeah."

The man lit a match with his hands cupped around it and touched the flame to the tobacco and smoke appeared.

"Have to get in the back. Front's full of newspapers," I said.

"Fine with me, man."

We leaned slightly and started toward the car. We scrunched our shoulders when the sheet of water from the roof of the building hit us. We ran a few steps, dodging puddles. I got into the driver's seat, and the man went around to the opposite side and got in the rear. We shivered and sat and closed our doors.

"Damn!"

We adjusted ourselves in the seats.

"Holy shit!"

"Mind if I smoke in here?"

"Naw," I said.

The man looked at the cigarette between two fingers and said, "Nasty shit. Smoke's some bad shit . . . you know it?"

"Yeah." I pulled the knob on the dash and the headlights came on bright against the building. The woman inside the restaurant looked up and stretched her neck, trying to see past the reflection on the inside of the big glass. She waved. I moved the gear lever and turned to look through the back window.

The man sucked on the cigarette. "My old lady told me smoking makes my breath smell like goat shit."

I finished backing and moved the gear lever down, then turned the steering wheel and eased James Louis toward the road in the darkness. "I smoke sometimes," I said.

"You got an extra joint?" the man asked.

"Sure." I put the coffee on the seat beside me and leaned forward and opened the ashtray and brought out a thinly rolled joint. I held it over my shoulder, passing it to the man in the back. I looked both ways and I pulled onto the road.

The windows on the front doors were down. The rest of the glass, rear, front, and sides, was damp from the fog and rain that blew through the holes in the front. The glass reflected the light of the headlamps. Outside was darkness, except in front where the headlamps showed the road and the faint lines of paint. A mailbox appeared off the shoulder on the right, and I eased the car to the right and off the shoulder. I stopped as close to the box as possible and, stretching, opened the front door of the mailbox and stuck a newspaper in the damp, dark hole.

"What you gonna do in Philadelphia?"

The man took a long, slow, deep drag on the joint, held his breath, then allowed the smoke to escape in snorts and blobs and little trickles. "Kill my old lady." I looked in the mirror. He was unbuttoning his pea coat.

I eased the car back onto the pavement and accelerated slowly.

"She's fucking my brother."

"Why don't you kill your brother?"

"I'm going to. I'm gonna kill both them motherfuckers." He took another drag on the joint and reached into the pea coat, into the bulky front that drooped open.

I turned to look toward the back. The man was sitting alongside bundles and grocery bags and wrappers from my snacks. He was holding a revolver. It was bluish and dull. It did not reflect any light.

"We're going to Philadelphia, man. Straight shot. No stopping."

I turned slowly toward the front. "I don't mind taking you to Philadelphia"—I looked at the gauges on the lighted dash—"but I need to deliver the rest of this stuff."

The man screamed, "Shut up!" He leaned forward from the back seat and stuck the barrel of the revolver in the soft place just behind my right ear. "Don't you even think about stoppin'! You understand? Huh?"

The man slid back in the seat and let the handle of the revolver rest on his knee, still pointed toward the front. He glanced to the side at his reflection in the glass, then beyond to the rain and the dark.

We rode for a while at a good clip but slow enough in the curves to be safe on the slick road, passing all the mailboxes where I was supposed to stop. I picked up the coffee and adjusted some of the bundles of newspapers on the seat beside me so I could rest and sit like in an armchair. I put the front windows up, and we rode in darkness except for the reflection of the dash lights and the headlamps. We passed the next truck stop, where the big trucks sat running, still and dark, and the sign next to the road flashed on and off: TWO LIVERMUSH BISCUITS $1.49. The sign could be hooked to a pick-up and towed somewhere else. In the creek bottom past the truck stop the leaves from the hardwoods, fresh from their fall, were solid on the road, stuck there by the rain.

"Why'd she leave?"

"Said I was fucked up." He took the last drag on the joint and put the roach in his mouth and chewed it and swallowed it. He still held the revolver pointed toward the front. He stared out the window.

We rode in silence, slowed for the curves and crossed the creeks in the middle of the bridges on the farm-to-market road.

"You know how I stayed alive for fourteen weeks?" he said. "I'd wait for a pile of gooks to come along—you know, hauling shit down the trail, chow and ammo—and I'd snatch the last one out of the pile and take all his stuff and choke his worthless little ass, then disappear before the rest of them knew *he* was gone. I got rice mostly, but some of them had 'C' rats, good old United States 'C' rats. Took 'em off one of us they'd blown away. But I got 'em back. They all had little bags of drugs. White powder or brown powder you could sniff or swallow and you'd get alert and strong like an animal. They always had good strong drugs. The drugs helped me keep moving."

I nodded my head.

He went on. "I made it back, and they said I ought to go to the rear for a while. When I was at the rear I found out my buddy got blown away while I was gone."

We were still in the dark of the car as we made our way down the hills and around the curves of the old road.

"Did you ever tell your wife what happened to you over there?"

"She didn't give a shit! Like my brother . . . yeah! That bastard! I shoulda killed him when we were little. Right before they stuck me in Laos I got a letter from my brother. They were havin' a party that night, him an' some of his college buddies. He said the ones that got high numbers in that fuckin' draft lottery were getting drunk to celebrate and the ones that got low numbers were getting drunk because they thought they were gonna get drafted and come to this place. Then they sent me out here in the fucking bush and my buddy got blown away while I was getting high off that stuff I got off those dead gooks. . . . He had a high number. That bastard got a high number. I shoulda killed that bastard when we were little."

The man relaxed in the back seat and took a moment to stare out the window. "Ain't no pussy in the world worth nothing! All they do is . . . they just . . . goddamn women . . . this place is so fucked up!"

When he raised the revolver to fire, I slammed on the brakes and spun the steering wheel to the left. The revolver fired into the roof as the man was thrown against the right rear door. Smoke and powder filled the inside of James Louis. We were in a skid to the right, going sideways; then as the man raised the revolver to fire again we hit the guard rail a glancing blow. The door beside the man sprung open. The man's head and arms went through the door glass. He was hanging out of the car where he had broken the glass. In the front I was braced by the bundles and the steering wheel and held my place. James Louis hit the guard rail again and bounce-stopped against the rail. I opened my door and jumped out. James Louis's engine was off and his left headlamp was on. A streak of light cut the rain. The man had been cut by the glass and was pinned between the rail and the car. I saw him raise his arm. A shot rang dull and muffled, like a thud. The shot removed the man's sock cap and most of his cranial vault.

The rain was heavy and water dripped from my bare head down my forehead, over my brows, into my eyes and beard; it tickled as it dripped. I wiped my face and beard.

Steam was coming from under the hood of James Louis. The right rear wheel was broken off where the man lay. The wheel was lying flat under the twisted guard rail. I pulled my jacket tight around me and pulled my collar up. I sat in the wet slice of light from the one headlamp on a part of the rail that was not damaged, and I waited.

It is almost five. The people will be coming soon with their produce, on the way to the markets in the city, and they will see me and they will stop to find out what has happened.

DATE DUE

MAY 5 '93			

HIGHSMITH   #LO-45227